VEIL OF DESTRUCTION

A KESSLER EFFECT NOVEL
BOOK THREE

VANNETTA CHAPMAN

Veil of Destruction

Requests for information should be addressed to: VannettaChapman (at) gmail (dot) com

Tennyson, Alfred Tennyson. "Ulysses." *The Poems of Alfred Lord Tennyson: 1830-1863*, George Routledge, London, 1906.

Cover design: Streetlight Graphics

First printing, 2023

ASIN : B0BL5KYNM8

ISBN: 9798394023446

Created with Vellum

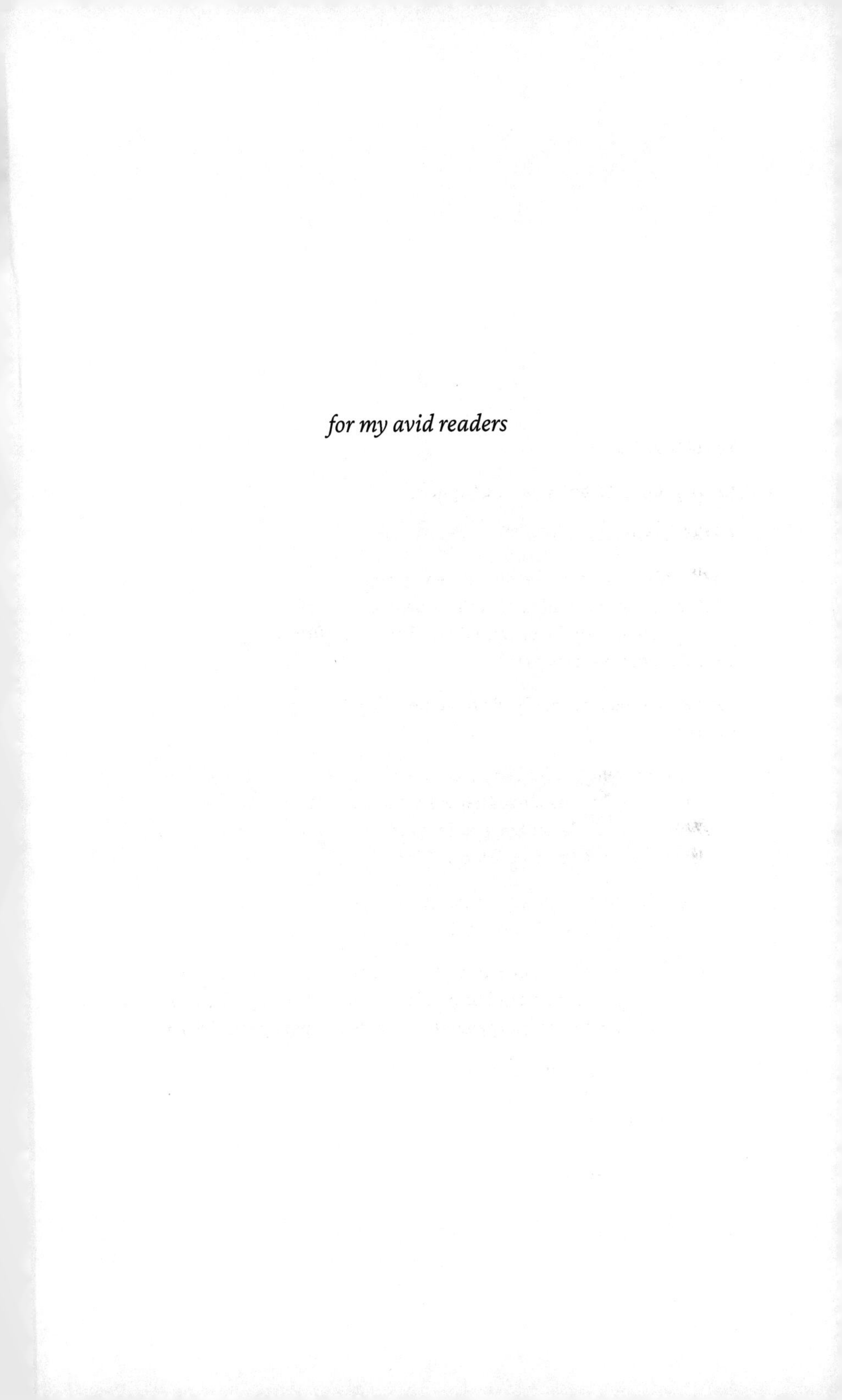

for my avid readers

"In three words I can sum up everything I've learned about life:
it goes on."
~Robert Frost

"That it will never come again is what makes life so sweet."
~Emily Dickinson

CHAPTER 1

The dream jolted Akule from sleep.

Redbird.

Torrential rain.

Blood.

Above, beyond, and through the images ran the overwhelming sense of grief and loss. She sat up, swiveled, placed her feet against the floor, and dropped her head into her hands. She no longer experienced the painful jolt back to reality—cell phones useless, communication nonexistent, food scarce, modern civilization a distant memory. She didn't even suffer through the sudden recollection that her mother had died. Those things her subconscious seemed to have accepted.

But her brother...how was she supposed to carry on never knowing what had happened to Paco? How could she possibly ignore the nagging feeling that he might be in trouble? That he might want to come home, but couldn't.

Was that what the dream meant?

She'd had it half a dozen times now. Redbird. Rain. Blood.

Grief. Loss. She ticked the items off on her fingers, stared at her hand, and made her decision.

She rose and dressed quickly. There wasn't much more she could put on. She'd slept in her clothes. They always slept in their clothes now. The cold was relentless. Pulling a cap over her raven black hair, gloves onto her hands, and a rain-resistant coat on, she stepped from her apartment into the predawn morning.

A north wind tore across the Chihuahuan desert.

The 27th of December would dawn like every other day had for the last week—weak sunlight or none at all, cold temperatures, more hardship.

Snow covered the surrounding mesas and continued to fall, though more lightly, more softly than the day before. Most of the citizens of Alpine—what was left of them—remained burrowed in their beds. At least they had beds.

It was early, too early, to be out. But what Akule had to do was best done before the sun came up. Also, she didn't care to spend another sleepless night second-guessing her decision. Then there was the dream. The possibility of experiencing that again was enough to drive her from her bed.

Akule had no doubt that her Aunt Tanda would be in her office. Tanda was the one person whose opinion she trusted. She trudged down the street, pushed open the door to the police station, and gave a small wave to Conor, who always seemed to be on the night shift.

"She in her office?"

"Sure is."

"I'll just—" Akule motioned toward the back, toward the office with *Police Chief* stenciled on the door.

Conor nodded and returned his attention to transcribing the previous day's call-outs in the journal Tanda insisted they keep. Of course, they weren't actual call-outs since no one's phone worked. A neighbor or family member would rush in asking for help and the officer on duty responded. Everything went into the journal.

The world might have changed.

The apocalypse might have come.

But Tanda Lopez was determined to be the defender of law and order.

Akule tapped lightly on the door, then turned the knob.

Tanda's expression broke into a smile at the sight of her niece. "Wow. You're up early."

"So are you."

Tanda shrugged that away and rose to pull her into a hug. Akule's aunt was on the short side—a good four inches shorter than Akule's five feet, eight inches. Tanda had been trim and toned even before food became scarce. Akule had always been thin too, but it had been a softer thinness before June 6th. Now she felt sinewy, as if everything that was extra had been chipped away by the harshness of winter in a post-modern world.

They both had straight black hair, though Tanda's was long and pulled back like their *abuela*, Akule's great-grandmother, had worn hers. Akule's had grown out to shoulder length. It was a different look for her. She preferred to chop it in a jagged style. Maybe that had been a small way to push back against the expectations of the world.

She no longer had the luxury of worrying about such things. It took all of her energy to merely survive each day.

Akule took the chair across from Tanda.

"Want some coffee?"

"No." Now that she was here, she didn't know how to begin. Perhaps she should have simply left in the middle of the night. It would have been easier. Though she loved her aunt and had no doubt that her aunt loved her, Tanda's piercing gaze caused her to squirm. Akule often wondered if Tanda had received their abuela's second sight. She certainly seemed to know what a person was thinking before they spoke.

As if to prove that very point, Tanda sat back in her chair and cradled her mug of coffee. Her first words were a statement, not a question. "You're leaving."

"I have to go look for him."

Tanda continued to study her, as if assessing whether she was up to this task. Finally, she nodded toward the window. "You could wait for the weather to clear."

"With no weather forecast, we have no idea when that will be."

"Why now?"

"Why not?"

"Where will you look?"

"I'll start in Cedar Hill. That's where he was living."

Tanda finally shifted her gaze, searched the opposite wall as if she could find the answer there. "I can't imagine what the Dallas area looks like now. I feel like I should go with you."

"You can't. We both know that. This town, what's left of it, depends on you."

"Paco is family. Family comes first." And then she surprised Akule with a confession. "We should have gone already. But it's been, you know...one hit after another."

First the battle with Marfa, then the battle with the Watchmen, then the winter and the flu season and even tighter food rations.

"Dad won't want me to go. That's why I'm telling you."

"We'll talk to him together."

"Do we have to?"

"Yeah. We do. He's on patrol at seven." Tanda glanced at the battery-operated wall clock.

Soon they'd be out of batteries, or they wouldn't recharge

from the solar panels. Then even the hours of the day would cease to hold any meaning.

"Only five-thirty," she said. "We can still catch him before his shift. Let's go."

They walked to the apartment that Keme had taken in Tanda's building, which was only a few blocks from the police station. He hadn't wanted to move into town. He'd wanted to stay in the trailer that Akule and Paco had been raised in, the trailer where the memories of her mother still saturated every corner of every room.

In the end, he'd accepted the practicality of moving into town. That admission and the fact that a crazed and armed drifter had tried to break into Tanda's apartment changed his mind. Tanda was fully capable of defending herself, but there'd been no stopping Keme then. He took the apartment two doors down. He'd wanted Akule to move in with him, but she'd assured him she was fine with her roommates.

She was fine with her roommates.

But she needed to bring her brother home.

She hoped her father would understand that. But whether he did or not, she was going.

Keme answered seconds after their knock, almost as if he'd been waiting for them. There had always been a strange kind of ESP between her dad and her aunt. She saw it now in the knowing glances they exchanged. She felt it in his sigh and Tanda's small shrug of her shoulders.

Her father stood nearly six feet tall. When Akule looked at him, she remembered her Kiowa heritage, which came from her grandmother. Her grandfather was Hispanic. They both still lived outside of Alpine, insisting they had what they needed on the small acreage that had been their home since before Keme was born.

"Better come in," Keme said.

They kept their coats on. The room was cold. Whoever had designed the building hadn't envisioned a time when there would be no heat or air conditioning. Open windows provided some relief in the summer, but during the winter...

Winter was simply a trial one fought to endure.

They sat around the dining room table. Someone else's home. Someone else's furniture. Some days it felt to her as if they'd taken up someone else's life. The original occupants of the apartment had been out of town on June 6th.

The day the satellites stopped working.

The day their entire world changed.

It wasn't only a matter of cell phones not working. Nearly every aspect of their daily lives had been dependent on 4G to one degree or another—shipping and receiving, manufacturing, GPS and signal lights, air traffic control towers, even train schedules. The train crash that occurred that first day still lay across the tracks that wound through Alpine.

The twisted pieces of metal acted as a sort of watershed in Akule's mind. There was before...when the tracks were clear for passage and the possibility of another life—a different life—lay just around the bend. And there was after...when every ounce of energy was focused on simply surviving.

"I'm going to find Paco."

"No, you're not."

"I am."

"We've talked about this. We agreed to wait until spring."

"I'm not waiting."

Akule's great-grandmother had been Kiowa. What percentage, Akule didn't know. Things like Ancestry.com no longer existed. Abuela had looked Indian. She had acted Indian. She had the stoicism of the Native Americans and the stubbornness of the Hispanic people. Abuela was old and diabetic and had been one of the first casualties.

But Akule saw her great-grandmother's traits in her father, and she felt those same traits in herself. Often they were like two trains colliding, neither willing nor able to change course. She was reminded again of the freight train and the Amtrak train. One had sideswiped the other. Their timing had been off by only a few seconds. The resulting crash killed eight and injured more.

Tanda seemed to sense the stalemate, so she cleared her throat and weighed in. "I'm sure you two could stare at one another all day, but I need to get back to work, Keme has patrol, and Akule...well, I'm not sure what you were supposed to do today."

"Helping Doc Cade, but I already told him I wouldn't be there."

"You told him you were leaving?" Keme sat back, raised and then lowered his hands as if to say *can you believe this girl?*

"I would like to side with you on this, Keme." Tanda cupped her hands, breathed into them, then stuck them into the pockets of her coat. "I don't like the idea of her going—"

"She's not."

"Or of her going alone."

"Definitely not."

"But I feel it too." Tanda sat forward. For a moment she stared down at the table, and Akule wondered if she was looking for the answers there. She shook her head once, then glanced from Akule to Keme. "I feel it too. Someone needs to go, and I don't...I just don't see how I can."

"Why now? Why not wait until spring?"

Akule was ready with her list of reasons, though she wouldn't tell him about the dream. Even to her ears, reciting a dream sounded like a child afraid of the boogeyman. She didn't have the words to explain that it wasn't merely a dream. Instead, she said, "There will be more people on the roads in the spring. There will be more danger in the spring. You said yourself that the roads are basically empty right now. We haven't had a drifter in what...a month?"

"Doesn't mean they aren't out there."

"I can take care of myself, Dad."

Keme exploded out of his chair, paced the short distance to the living area and back. "How would you even get there?"

"I'll take my mare."

"You'll need a pack animal too. You'll need grain for the mare and supplies for yourself." Tanda sat up straighter, crossed her arms, stuck her hands under her armpits as if to warm them.

"It's a long trip, Akule. I know you're strong. You've matured a lot in the last six months, and if anyone can find Paco *and his family...*" She emphasized the last three words as if Akule had forgotten about her two nephews and sister-in-law. "If anyone can find them, I believe you can. But traveling five hundred miles on horseback in the dead of winter won't be easy."

"I don't expect it to be."

"Say you can make thirty miles a day. That's a little more than two weeks to get there, plus time to find them, and then a two-week return trip. Returning will be harder. You can't load the entire family on the back of your mare."

"And you're not even sure he'll be there." Keme sat at the table again, concern and heartache coloring his expression.

Akule understood what that was about.

She understood that her father had lost his grandmother, his wife, and countless friends. Maybe he thought it was better to hold on to the one child he had with him rather than risk her being killed in the search for the rest of his family. He might have felt that way, but that wasn't what he said.

"You think I don't want to go? You think I wouldn't have

left the day we understood nothing was going back to normal? Or the day your mother died?" He dropped his head, and that sign of grief tore at Akule's heart more than his words. Finally he raised his gaze to hers. "The safest thing, the smartest thing, is to wait here. Paco knows where we are. He'll get here when he can."

"I can't wait for that, Dad. I can't do the safe thing. What's the point in trying so hard to stay alive if we're not going to at least attempt to save the people we love?"

Keme didn't have an answer to that.

Tanda rubbed her temples with her fingertips.

"Headache?" Akule asked.

Tanda waved away the question and addressed her next comment to Keme. "We can't stop her. She'll go with or without your permission. She's only telling us because she respects you."

Akule didn't like being talked about as if she weren't there, but she also appreciated Tanda stating the obvious. She would go with or without her father's permission.

Then Tanda played the card that hit home. "Lucy would agree with her. In fact, she would have insisted that you go months ago. I know it, and you know it."

All of the argument went out of her dad at the mention of her mother's name.

"Fine."

Akule breathed out a sigh of relief.

"But I'm going with you."

"Dad, I don't need you with me. I don't want you with me."

"It doesn't matter what you want, Akule. I'm going."

Tanda nodded as if she'd expected as much. Why hadn't Akule seen this coming? She should have simply left town. She could be five miles north by now. Five miles closer to her brother.

But another voice, a smaller voice, pushed to the front of her thoughts. That voice was soft, convincing. It was, she supposed, the voice of her mother.

Why not go with your dad?

Why do you feel a need to do this alone?

She didn't have an answer to either of those questions.

"Forty-eight hours," Tanda said. "Let me see what supplies I can get from Stan and arrange for some kind of pack animal. You can both ride your mares. Take something to trade for two more horses once you get there. That should be enough. The kids are still small—they can double up with Paco and Claire."

Tanda stood as if it was settled.

They all stood.

It was settled. Akule would leave in forty-eight hours, and she wouldn't be going alone.

Akule's father surprised her then. He pulled her into his arms, then reached out and pulled Tanda into the circle. They stood there, the three of them, and Akule understood that she would hold onto this image until she was back in Alpine again.

And she was coming back. But she'd come back with her brother, his wife, and both their children. She wasn't going to settle for anything less.

CHAPTER 2

Keme made it to his patrol assignment fifteen minutes early. He was to ride the northwest circuit around town. Highway 118 to past the airport, over to County Road 1703, south to 67, then east into town. Once there, he'd take a fifteen-minute break, then ride the route in reverse.

There were four people on patrol at all times. Their routes and times were staggered. To someone watching, it would look haphazard. It was anything but. The Council had spent several days hammering out the details of the protection of Alpine. The last thing they wanted to be was predictable.

Being predictable could get you and those you loved killed.

Highway 118 was, as usual, deserted—absolutely no movement as far as he could see. The airport continued to mock them. Since the day the satellites fell, since June 6th, no planes had landed on the small airfield. As for the planes usually stored there, their owners had fled within the first week. No one had returned. No movement on CR 1703.

Alpine remained an isolated island in the middle of the Chihuahuan Desert.

Keme used the time he rode to create a supply list in his mind. At least it kept his thoughts off the cold. The temperatures wouldn't be so bad, but the wind from the north caused his bones to ache—another sign that he was getting old.

When he'd completed his fourth circuit, he checked in at the Sul Ross campus where Stan Makowski was coordinating patrols. Tanda insisted on rotating personnel in and out of each position *just in case*. Their entire life had turned into one huge *just in case*.

Surprisingly, you got used to it.

"Got a minute before you go?" Stan nodded toward what had been the rodeo office. Sul Ross was a small-sized, public university that had served the Big Bend region of far West Texas. A founding member of the National Intercollegiate Rodeo Association, the school's arena, stalls, and offices had proven a perfect fit for Tanda's Strategic Command Center.

Keme followed Stan into an office that was only marginally warmer than the outdoors.

"Tanda caught me up on what's happening."

Instead of responding, Keme sank into a chair.

"Let's go over what you and Akule might need."

"We'll both take our mares—if you can spare them."

"Yes, we can. Be sure you bring them back." Stan attempted a smile, then frowned down at a sheet of paper he'd been scribbling on. "Logan wants to give both mares a thorough going over. As for a pack animal, the Scotts have half a dozen mules. Mike's planning on using them in the spring to put some crops in the ground. He's willing to send one with you."

"All right."

"I've set aside a minimal amount of feed for the animals. You're going to have to find more along the way."

Keme nodded. Animal feed was already on his mental list.

"I can also send K-rations—enough for two weeks. Again,

that won't be enough for the entire trip, but it'll at least get you there."

"Medical kit?"

"Yup. Already cleared it with Cade." Stan sat back in his chair and studied Keme.

It was strange for Keme to realize he'd barely known the man before June 6th. They'd both grown up in Alpine and gone to the same school though Keme was a few years older. Stan had worked for Tanda for at least half a dozen years, but it had taken the apocalypse for Keme and him to form a friendship. Maybe that's the way things went. Maybe you didn't grow close to another person until you really needed them...until you held each other's life in your hands.

They'd fought beside each other.

They'd defended Alpine.

Essentially, they were brothers.

"How are you doing for ammunition?"

"Half a box of shells for my rifle. About the same for the handgun."

Stan stretched his neck to the right, then the left. "Let's hope you don't end up in a situation where you need more than that. You leave Friday morning?"

"Before daybreak, if I know my daughter."

They stood, walked out of the office and toward the arena.

"How are the kids?" Keme asked.

"Good. School is closed until this weather passes through. Zoey's a champ though. She's somehow managing to stay sane with four children cooped up in the living room."

"It's fortunate you have a fireplace."

"It is indeed." Stan pulled him into a hug, which conveyed the things they didn't say, then stepped back. "Don't worry about your shift tomorrow. I've got someone to cover it. Take the day to get packed."

Keme didn't think it would take a day to pack, but he nodded his appreciation.

He walked over to Akule's apartment. Akule's roommate, Emily, opened the door.

"You're bundled up."

"And I'm still cold." She ushered him in, slammed the door shut, and pushed a pile of old towels up against the bottom of the door. "Helps keep the draft out."

"Maybe you should think about moving home—at least until the weather changes."

"No way. Akule, Briley, and I are independent women."

At the sound of her name, Akule peered out from her bedroom. "Are you packed?"

"We're not leaving until Friday morning."

"Uh-huh." She ducked back into her room.

Emily shrugged. "Good luck on your trip, Mr. Lopez. I hope you find your son." Then she walked into her bedroom, quietly shutting the door behind her.

"She's worried I'm not coming back." Akule sat on her bed and motioned Keme toward her desk chair.

"It is a possibility."

"I know that, Dad." She shook her head. "On the one hand, I'm relieved you're going with me, but on the other...I'm not so sure this is a good idea."

"Might as well stick with relieved, since I'm going either way."

"Yeah. That's kinda what I figured." She pushed a pile of socks closer to her backpack. "Now that it's certain we're going, I can't seem to make up my mind on what to take. I've thought this through so many times...but now I keep questioning myself."

"Give me an example."

"Three pairs of socks or four?"

"Four."

"Two sets of gloves?"

"Yes. Wear one. Pack an extra set."

They worked their way through the piles of stuff on her bed, separating them into *take* and *leave* piles. She only overruled him once, when he said she should leave Lucy's letters. "No room for sentimental items, Akule. Paco can read those when he gets home."

"Yeah, I hear you." She thumbed through the envelopes.

Lucy had written to Paco once a week after the events of June 6th, even though there had been no way to send the letters. She had said that she wanted her son to know she'd been thinking about him. She had teased that when they were all together again, he would be free to laugh at how sentimental she'd become in her old age.

Old age. She'd died a week before her forty-sixth birthday. Died in the battle with Marfa. When he allowed his thoughts to linger on that—on the gaping hole in his life, he felt himself teetering on the edge of a very dark, very deep chasm. He couldn't allow himself the luxury of grief right now. He'd been grieving, for months. He suspected he would continue to do so for the rest of his life. But for this moment, for the next few weeks, he would put his grief aside and concentrate on his daughter and son.

He ran his fingers across her handwriting, then nodded. Akule pushed the letters into the bottom of her pack.

Keme cleared his throat. "We need to talk about our route."

"Why?"

"Because we need to think this through."

"We've both driven to Dallas many times, Dad."

"Nothing is the same as it was before. We need to view our route with that in mind." Keme pulled a state map from his pocket and spread it out on the floor.

Akule joined him there, running her finger from Alpine, past Fort Stockton, to Interstate 20, then northeast toward the Dallas area.

"I see three problems with that route. Three things we should avoid—Fort Stockton, I-20, and Ft. Worth."

"Okay. What's your idea?"

He traced a route southeast to Dryden, north to Sheffield, across Interstate 10 west of Ozona and finally north to San Angelo.

"How do we know San Angelo is any better than Fort Stockton?"

"We don't." Keme reached into his pocket again and pulled out a folded, letter-sized envelope with a crude map penned on the back. "Franklin gave me this before he left."

"Your neighbor Franklin?"

"The same."

"Kinda big guy with an even bigger mutt? Used to sit out on his porch drinking beer?"

Keme hadn't had a drink in seven years. He still considered himself an alcoholic. In his way of thinking, it was the same as saying he was tall with black hair. The defect in his genetic makeup was a part of who he was. It was something he would always have to stand guard against. That was one thing that hadn't changed since June 6th.

"Franklin was a good guy, and he was prepared when he left. The route he was taking, the route he thought was safest because of things he'd heard over his short wave, was 90 east to Dryden and then Highway 349 north. Cross I-10 where Highway 290 intersects it west of Ozona. Those were all small towns before June 6th. Chances are they're even smaller now."

"Or nonexistent."

"Exactly."

"I guess it's farther?"

"A little. Less chance of being killed for the food in our packs."

"Okay. Does this mean we're stopping in San Angelo? Stopping at..." She spun the envelope around to face her, looked closer at Franklin's map, and scowled. "At Franklin's in-law's?"

"I don't know. We can decide that when we get close."

"Why would we?"

"They might be able to shed some light on the situation to the north. At least we wouldn't be going in blind."

"Fair enough."

Keme stood and walked to the door, but Akule called him back. "Thanks, Dad."

"For what?"

"For not treating me like a child. For asking my opinion about things."

He studied her, almost settled for a nod, but then he thought of Lucy. Thought of how he still grieved the things he hadn't said. "Your opinion matters, and you're not a child."

She pulled in her bottom lip and nodded.

"They're having a send-off for us tomorrow night."

"What? We don't have time for that."

"Actually we do, and folks...there are some things you do because other people need you to do it. They need to say goodbye. They need to believe we'll come back."

"We will."

"I know it." Grinning he added, "Six o'clock tomorrow. Tanda's. Be there or she'll come looking for you."

CHAPTER 3

Dylan had half a mind to simply follow Keme and Akule out of town. Make himself known twenty miles out when it would be harder for them to send him back. Hell, he wasn't a UPS package, and he wasn't going back. But what was the best way to make them see it from his perspective?

He was walking home from his patrol on Thursday morning when he saw Akule step out of the triage center, which was what they called the building that had housed the train station.

No more trains.

Didn't need a station.

Hence the triage center.

Akule nodded a greeting and walked past him as if he were some stranger on the road. He pivoted and caught up with her. "You're in a hurry."

"Lots to do."

"Because of your trip."

"Yeah."

"I'm going with you."

She stopped so abruptly, he shot past her. He turned around and walked back to where she was waiting with both hands on her hips.

"No, you're not."

"Yes, I am."

"What is wrong with you, Dylan? This is a family thing, and you're not family."

If she thought she could hurt his feelings and he'd scuttle away, then Akule Lopez was sorely mistaken. He'd been in the same grade as her in school, though he was a year older. His mother referred to his sophomore year in high as his *lost year*, always spoken with emphasis as if it should be italicized. In truth, he'd simply been angry that his dad left. He'd rebelled in every way he could think of, including but not limited to failing all of his classes.

That lost year taught him a lot. Mostly, it had taught him that he didn't want to be a loser. He wanted to be a winner, and after that he was. When he repeated his sophomore year, everything was dramatically different.

His life became grades and football. He earned the spot for starting quarterback his junior year, and in his senior year he helped take the Alpine Bucks to their first state championship. He didn't do it alone, but he helped. That was enough in his mind. He'd graduated with academic honors and an invitation to play ball at Sam Houston State. He passed on the football scholarship because he'd done what he'd set out to do. He'd made up for his *lost year*.

But he'd never left Alpine.

He'd planned to. Didn't every kid plan to leave their hometown? One thing had led to another, and then June 6th happened. That was nearly seven months ago and he was still stuck in Alpine. Going with Akule might be his only chance to break free, and he wasn't about to waste it.

"Maybe you're not the only one who wants out of this town. Did you ever think of that?"

"We're not going on vacation."

She stepped closer, close enough that he could see how remarkable her eyes were—dark brown pools of mystery, fathomless. He also saw the dark skin beneath her eyes. She needed him, whether she knew it or not.

"We're going to find my brother."

"I heard your pop was going with you."

"Yes. And two is plenty."

"Not really. Liam says three is the best number, for night watches and such." Liam Contreras was former military and had arrived in Alpine with Harper and Cade. Dylan had spent many hours quizzing Liam about life *Out There*. "He's one of the few people in this town who's actually been out there since June 6th."

"Are you forgetting about Harper and Cade?"

"No, and they both agree that I should go...that three is better than two."

"You talked to Harper and Cade?" She looked like she was going to punch him. She didn't, but he suspected she wanted to. Instead, she stuck her hands in her pockets and strode off toward her apartment.

It was the wrong direction from his mom's house, but he followed her anyway. "Why do you have to be so stubborn?"

"I'm being stubborn?"

"Yes. You should be glad I want to go."

"But I'm not."

"I'm going anyway."

"You do what you need to do, Dylan." She walked away, muttering words like *unwanted, unneeded, unnecessary*.

Dylan smiled and turned back in the opposite direction. Akule might think she didn't want him with her, but that would change when she saw how tough it was *Out There* on the road. He'd listened to all of Liam's stories, and Liam hadn't held anything back. He'd been on the wrong side of things until he realized it and switched to the right side of things. Dylan admired the man. It took guts to admit you were wrong.

Liam said there was no time to waste on false pretenses.

He also said that maybe he'd been there for a reason, that Harper and Cade had needed him even though they didn't realize it. Without Liam, Harper would have bled out in the back of the jeep they were driving. Instead, they'd rescued two kids and Harper was going to have a baby before spring. Even Cade admitted that they'd needed Liam, that without him things would have been much, much worse.

And that had sealed it for Dylan.

He was going with Akule. He'd always had a little bit of a crush on her. From a distance. She was out of his league. She was alarmingly beautiful, did not care what other people thought, and had never spared him a second glance. During their high school years, Dylan had been all about winning the approval of his classmates.

He'd needed it back then.

Since June 6th, he wasn't sure what he needed.

This was his chance though. To shake off the dust of Alpine. To rescue someone. To do something that mattered. He was going with Akule. He'd known it the moment he'd heard that she was leaving.

Actually, he was surprised she hadn't left already. She struck him as an action-first, think-about-it-later kind of person. And those kinds of people were needed, or things would never get done.

Unwanted, unneeded, unnecessary.

It didn't really bother him that she didn't want him.

And maybe in the end, his tagging along would prove to be unneeded and unnecessary. No harm, no foul.

What wasn't okay was for him to stay in Alpine where things were relatively safe and everyone was waiting out winter. Not while she was on the road looking for family.

He'd already spoken with her father, something he wasn't about to admit to her. Keme had looked at Dylan with that unreadable expression he was known for, then shrugged and said, "You're going to be the one to tell her."

Mission accomplished.

Now all he needed to do was go home and tell his own mother. It wasn't like he needed her permission. He was twenty-three years old, after all. But June 6th had changed things. Changed his perspective. Changed what could and couldn't happen in the future. If he were killed on the road, he didn't want his mother's last memory of him to be a note on his pillow.

A child would sneak out without a word.

But Dylan Spencer wasn't a child anymore. He was a man now, and he'd have the uncomfortable conversation because it was the right thing to do.

Then he'd spend the rest of the afternoon packing.

AKULE DID NOT WANT to go to Tanda's on Thursday evening, but she understood that not going would hurt her aunt.

"We'll go with you," Emily said.

"That way it won't be all old people." Briley wiggled her eyebrows. "Maybe we can sneak away and hang with some of our friends. After you put in an appearance."

Akule didn't know what she'd done to deserve two good roommates. She'd spent some time stumbling around the state before she'd settled down in Alpine. She'd slept on people's couches. She'd even slept on park benches. Sometimes the park benches were the better option.

But Emily and Briley were the real deal.

Emily had long, wavy, brown hair and always wore jeans, a western shirt, and a large belt buckle. She could have been on a poster for *Visit Alpine*. She also could have been all-star rodeo, if school hadn't been permanently dismissed the previous June. She'd been cheated out of her senior year and her shot at fame. Both were things she shrugged off as if they hadn't been her childhood dream. They had. She had the posters on the walls of her bedroom to prove it—Chris LeDoux, Ty Murray, and Wylee Brown.

Instead of rodeoing, she was interning with Logan Wright, who spent half his time in his pre-apocalypse profession as a veterinarian and half his time helping Doc Turner and Cade Dawson at the triage center working on people.

Briley was blonde, willowy, and thoughtful. She had hoped to publish a novel. Now she was working on the Legacy Project, an attempt to record what had happened and what was still happening to their world.

The three of them looked like the most unlikely of friends.

But Briley and Emily had become like sisters to Akule. She didn't mind spending her last evening in Alpine with them, even if it was at her aunt's with a bunch of old people.

She was surprised to find Tanda's apartment practically overflowing with friends and family. Her grandparents, her father and aunt, and everyone who was on the Council—the folks who had been elected to make decisions for Alpine. Tanda and Keme were on the Council. Some of the other council members Akule liked very much—Doc Miles, Logan, Fire Chief Dixie Peters, and Harper Moore who was married to Doc Cade. Some of the Council who were there she didn't really know except to nod at when they passed on the street—Ron, Emmanuel, and an old guy named Gonzo.

Akule suppressed a groan because these people were obviously here for her dad, but then she saw her group in a back corner of the room. They were sitting on the floor and crowded in together to make room for Akule, Emily, and Briley. She felt like a pup in a litter, but it was a good feeling. The feeling of dread that seemed to accompany her everywhere lessened then faded away completely. Unfortunately, Dylan was part of the litter—wavy brown hair imprinted with the cowboy hat he usually wore, laughing at something someone said, then turning and piercing her with those dark brown eyes.

For once he didn't set her nerves on edge. Maybe he simply didn't have time to, as Cade stepped to the front of the room and raised his hands for folks to quiet down.

"If I'd known thirty bodies could raise the temperature of a room this much, I'd have invited you all to my house."

Everyone laughed, and Akule unzipped her coat. Cade was right. It was at least ten degrees warmer than usual.

"We're here tonight to give a send-off to Akule, Keme, and Dylan."

So everyone knew about Dylan. There were certainly no gasps of surprise. Akule noticed his mother, Virginia Spencer, sitting beside Tanda. Yeah, everyone knew. This was happening, whether she was happy about it or not.

Cade motioned for the three of them to join him up front.

"This is worse than standing in front of a class in high school," Akule muttered, but her friends pushed her forward.

"You three will be in our thoughts...and our prayers... until we see you riding back into town. We understand your need to find your family, to bring them home." His gaze jumped to Harper, whose stomach seemed to grow larger every day. Jack and Olivia Donovan, the two children they'd rescued from

Guadalupe Peak, sat on either side of her in the overstuffed chair.

Cade's voice took on a more somber tone. "We understand the dangers you'll face, and the sacrifice you're making. Stan has assured me you're well equipped."

"Even found them a mountaineering tent, though I doubt you'll be finding any mountains between here and Dallas." This from Stan, who Akule thought was attempting to lighten the mood, but his voice caught on the last word, and he brushed at his eyes.

"Just as important as the supplies that you'll take are the supplies you'll need to trade for, and that's one reason we're here tonight. The people assembled here wanted a chance to give what you might need."

A silence pervaded the room as one by one, folks made their way forward and placed their offering in a box that Tanda had slid in front of them. A gold watch from Ron. A harmonica from her grandfather. Everyone laughed when Logan offered an unopened bottle of whiskey. "No one's making this anymore. It should trade well."

Packs of cigarettes, a jar of honey, a knitted baby blanket from her grandmother, a diamond ring. The young people from Akule's group gave a tin of Skoal, a pouch of chewing tobacco, an intricately beaded bracelet, a paperback novel.

All things from the world that had existed before.

All things that were becoming increasingly difficult, or even impossible, to find.

Akule was overwhelmed by their generosity.

She didn't know what to say to these people. She didn't know how to express what their gifts, their presence, meant to her. Fortunately her father found the right words.

"As you all know, we are going to find my son, Paco. Our plan, our hope, is to bring him back, to bring his wife Claire, and my grandsons Pete and Danny home." His face was stoic, but his voice...his voice held emotion that Akule thought he'd long ago learned to keep from his expression.

She stepped closer to him, so that their shoulders were touching. She tried to give him some of her strength.

"We are grateful for what you have sacrificed here. And we pledge that we will bring back what the people of Alpine need most—information on what has happened, news on what is to come, details of possible trade routes."

Everyone nodded in agreement.

Akule was suddenly painfully aware of the isolation they had endured. The lack of information was maddening. The lack of contact with other people was sometimes as difficult to bear as the lack of food and medicine. They needed to know what was happening in the world beyond their corner of Texas. And maybe that was another thing that had driven her to insist they leave.

Alpine was a good place.

In many ways it was a safe place.

But no community was meant to exist in total isolation.

Tanda moved in front of everyone, holding a book.

Holding the book Akule's mother had loved so much. It was battered, with one corner torn from the cover. The back cover had been taped on where it was tearing loose. Akule had looked through it many times. She'd read her mother's notes in the margins. Fingered the dog-eared pages. Envisioned her mother teaching in front of a class of college students.

"As many of you know, Lucy was a literature professor and a great lover of poetry."

"Oh, boy..." Dylan said, and everyone laughed.

Even Akule.

Even her father.

"It seems appropriate to send you off with these words, with this blessing." Tanda stared down at the open book.

Akule thought she must be gathering her fears close, covering them in Tennyson's words.

Death closes all; but something ere the end,
Some work of noble note, may yet be done...
Come, my friends,
'Tis not too late to seek a newer world.
Push off, and sitting well in order smite
The sounding furrows; for my purpose holds. .

.

Tanda reached for Akule and pulled her close. She stood there, eyes closed, heart open to the words of her mother's favorite poem. Tanda on her left. Her father standing close on her right. This was her family, but there was more family that she hadn't held in far too long. That was why they were going.

To sail beyond the sunset, and the baths
Of all the western stars, until I die.
It may be that the gulfs will wash us down;
It may be we shall touch the Happy Isles,
And see the great Achilles, whom we knew.

Akule closed her eyes against the words that were coming. The same words that her father had recited over her mother's grave.

Though much is taken, much abides; and though

We are not now that strength which in old days
Moved earth and heaven, that which we are, we are—
One equal temper of heroic hearts,
Made weak by time and fate, but strong in will
To strive, to seek, to find, and not to yield.

The room was absolutely still. Then Emily said, "Professor Lopez is smiling down on us. She always thought poetry could cure just about any problem."

There were nods of agreement and murmurs of "Godspeed." People slowly made their way out of the apartment, as if they were unwilling to see this night end.

Suddenly Akule's grandparents stood in front of her.

"Take care of your father," her grandfather said.

"You are very brave, Akule. You remind me of *mi madre*. You have her strength. Her gifts." Her grandmother pulled her into a hug, kissed her face, then held her at arm's length. "Give my great-grandchildren my love and tell them that I will make a wonderful meal to celebrate their return."

Tears slipped down Akule's face as she hugged these two people who had been such an important part of her life. When they'd gone, she glanced around the room. Her group had left, giving her time with her family. Dylan sat next to his mother, holding his Stetson, turning it in his hands as if he might find answers embossed on the brim. His mother was plainly trying to curtail her emotions.

Akule wondered again why he was doing this. What was

the real reason? She decided it didn't matter. He was right. Three was a better number than two.

Keme pulled out the map, showed Tanda and Dylan and Virginia the route they'd decided on. Virginia asked a few questions. When Dylan and his mom stood to go, Akule heard the woman say to her father, "Please bring him home. He's all I have."

Ten minutes later it was only herself, her father, and her aunt. They stood on Tanda's patio, looking out into the night. There were no lights. Even now, six months after the event, the darkness of things took Akule by surprise.

She thought of her dream, and she pushed the memory of it away. Finally she was doing something, and doing something was always better than doing nothing. Or so it seemed to her. She supposed they would soon test the truth of that.

Test it, and be tested by it.

CHAPTER 4

They left before first light.

The snow had stopped, but the temperatures remained low and cloud cover obscured any light from the moon or stars. Only Tanda and Logan were there to see them off. Everyone else had said what needed to be said the previous evening.

Logan gave Akule a few last-minute instructions about the horses and the emergency medical kit.

Tanda assured Dylan that they would check in on his mom.

Keme didn't know if his stomach was teetering from nerves, worry, or excitement. Maybe all three. He adjusted his position in the saddle. "An Indian riding a horse...just like old times."

"Never forget that you're a computer specialist. That may still come in handy someday." Tanda patted the mare's neck. "Be careful. Don't take any unnecessary risks. Patrols will keep an eye out for you."

"It would be good if they didn't shoot us on our way back into town," Dylan said.

"We'll be a larger group returning, so we should be easy to

spot." Akule said the words with complete confidence.

Keme realized his daughter had always been like that—unwavering, resolute, without doubt. When she was certain of a thing, there was no persuading her it might turn out differently.

"It'll be a month, maybe longer," Keme reminded her.

And then they turned and made their way out of town. It was early, and the sound of their horses echoed through the empty streets of Alpine. Though the streets were vacant, the town wasn't actually deserted. There was a lot of life left in the small town situated on the high plateau—Davis Mountains to the north, Chisos Mountains to the south, Chihuahua Desert covering the area in between.

Keme thought they'd made a stand against all that had happened in the last six months. They'd stood together and survived, but at a terrible cost. So many dead—some from the battles they'd fought, others from the scarcity they endured. Those who had survived were weary. As he and Akule and Dylan made their way out of town, most of the residents of Alpine slept.

Exhausted from the day before.

Needing all the rest they could get for the day ahead.

As they rode northeast, Keme resisted the urge to look back. They traveled along the side of Highway 90. It was thirty miles to Marathon. Keme didn't want to push the horses, but he did want to see what they were able to do. If they needed to adjust their timeframe, better to realize it on the first day out.

Keme rode the mare he'd used for patrol the last six months. Amber was a chestnut Morgan with a sweet disposition.

The saddle mule the Scotts had loaned them stood thirteen hands tall. Brown, sturdy, and sure-footed, Fiona had no trouble keeping up with the horses.

Akule rode a dapple gray with a bad attitude. She'd taken on the challenge of training the horse in the late fall, when everyone had had their fill of the mare. The horse kicked, nipped and fought the bit—for everyone except Akule. She had a way with the mare that Keme did not understand.

Dylan rode a bay Quarter Horse. Of course he did. Quarter Horses had long been the premier rodeo horse, and Keme knew the boy had been active in local rodeos after finishing high school.

Not a boy.

Dylan was a man, or he wouldn't be traveling with them.

And his daughter was a woman.

Time certainly marched on.

Five miles outside of town, sunlight splashed across the desert floor, and the road took a turn toward the southeast. They passed a few abandoned cars, some with bullet holes in their doors and windshields. The vehicles had plainly been stripped of anything useful, and no one suggested they stop to investigate.

There were no signs of people—no bodies either.

They surprised three does grazing in the bar ditch, and all pulled their horses to a stop. Dylan held up his arms as if he were holding a bow, pulling it tight, letting it fly. Akule rolled her eyes, but Keme smiled. He liked Dylan's attitude. The young man seemed to have adjusted to the realities of the new world that Keme still struggled against.

When Keme figured they'd reached the fifteen-mile mark, he nodded toward a stand of mesquite trees.

They dismounted, winding the lead ropes over the branches of the trees. Dylan and Akule checked the horses' hooves while Keme pulled out his binoculars and glassed the area around them. Nothing but desert, as far as the eye could see.

He hadn't realized how freeing it would feel to leave Alpine behind them. He'd always been happy living in the town where he'd grown up, and he still was. He supposed if the satellite array were replaced and the computers booted up, he would live there still.

And yet, the burden he'd been carrying since June 6th lightened a bit as they put Alpine behind them. Yes, he felt responsible for Dylan and Akule. But the weight of the town was out of his hands. The responsibility for its citizens was no longer his. At least for a time.

More important than what he didn't feel was what he did feel.

Hope.

Hope was beginning to blossom in his heart.

That he might actually find his son.

That he would see his daughter-in-law.

That he would hold his grandchildren.

"Your horse just nipped mine." Dylan stood with his hands on his hips, frowning at Akule's mare. "What's her name? Grendel?"

"I believe you're thinking of Grendel's mom."

"Monster, cave, trolls and giants, blood and carnage."

"Yeah. Beowulf is the hero, but Grendel is referred to as a male. You're thinking of Grendel's mom."

"No name?"

"Not that I remember."

"Huh. Amazing the stuff you forget once you've passed senior English." He pulled off his cowboy hat and slapped it against his leg. "So what's your horse's name?"

"Daisy."

"Daisy?"

"Yes. Daisy."

"That name does not fit that horse."

"What's your horse's name?"

"Texas Lady."

Akule laughed.

"I call her Tex."

"Okay. Well, it's your horse, so..."

Keme rather enjoyed seeing his daughter interact with someone her age. He realized he knew very little about her. Rather, he knew little about the adult person that she'd become. Akule had put both him and Lucy through a few rough years while she "found herself." Perhaps that was why he relished seeing that she'd turned into a functioning adult.

Not that he said as much.

"Ten minutes left of our lunch break. You two going to gab or eat?"

"I can do both at once," Dylan boasted.

Akule shook her head, then said, "I'm headed to the ladies' room." She walked in the opposite direction and turned behind a clump of cacti. When she came back, they ate jerky, shared a package of dried apricots, and topped it off with plenty of water.

Keme studied the horizon. Deserted. Covered with snow. No sign of life at all. "Hopefully there will be more water in Marathon."

"Hopefully there will be some frozen pizzas in the freezer of the Gage Hotel." Dylan pulled himself up and into the saddle, then adjusted the brim of the Stetson. "I could use a pepperoni with extra cheese right now."

"Right. Pizza." Akule's words dripped with sarcasm, but she was smiling. "Electricity's been out for six months, but you keep dreaming, cowboy."

They came across the first bodies two hours later.

DYLAN HAD SEEN plenty of bodies since June 6th.

He'd witnessed the initial carnage at the train crash that happened the moment the satellites went off-line, which meant all GPS was offline, which resulted in the crash between the passenger train from Marfa and the freight train from Fort Stockton. The Alpine police and fire department handled the situation, but the townspeople watched from a distance.

Dylan had watched from a distance.

The following weeks had been an adjustment period for everyone. Death became something they dealt with because there was no other choice. It was nothing like the video games he'd played as a teen. It seemed to Dylan that in this real-life battle that had been forced upon them no one won. You simply existed to struggle through another day.

By the time Alpine defended itself against the citizens of Marfa, who had attacked in the hopes of stealing what little supplies they had, Dylan had been a part of the defense. Since then, he'd become a regular part of the perimeter patrol. He—hell, not just him but everyone his age—had been forced to take a crash course in being an adult.

The apocalypse had arrived.

It wasn't a game.

It wasn't a movie.

It was their life.

Dylan would have said that he was used to it. That nothing could surprise him. He was wrong. The sight of the body behind the wheel and the body in the passenger seat of the SUV vehicle in the middle of the road caused his stomach to clinch in a fist.

"Why would they have stayed in the vehicle?" Akule rode her horse closer to the vehicle.

The tires had been taken. The back seat cut open. The trunk

pilfered. Even parts of the engine were gone. But the two bodies in the front seats—those had been left.

"Maybe they were afraid to leave the vehicle," Dylan suggested.

"They could have been sick, run out of gas, didn't think they could walk to the next town." Keme raised his eyes to the horizon, to Marathon. "We need to keep going."

An hour later, they pulled into what was left of Marathon.

Gateway to Big Bend National Park.

Second largest town in Brewster County, which wasn't saying much. The population hovered near 450 in the best of times. Based on what he was seeing, the population today was zero. Dylan had been to Marathon many times. He'd even taken his date for senior prom to the restaurant at the Gage. A dozen of them had gone—including Akule.

As they rode into town via Highway 90, the sounds of their horses' hooves against the pavement echoed through the deserted streets. The sound was eerie. The quiet was unnerving.

They passed the motel & RV park—deserted.

The Gage Wellness Spa—deserted.

And pulled up in front of the Gage Hotel—deserted.

"Why's everything named Gage?" he asked.

Akule's voice was low, matter-of-fact, reminding him of their history teacher. "American rancher from the turn of the century."

"Like year two thousand?"

"Like year nineteen hundred. His ranch once included 500,000 acres."

"That explains why they named everything in town after him."

What had been the most iconic hotel in the Texas south-west looked as if it had been ransacked. Much of the building was constructed from adobe, but any portions of the building that could burn had. The fountain in front of the hotel had been toppled over. Bullets had shattered most of the windows.

"Akule, ride a perimeter around the hotel. Don't go inside —yet. Dylan, I want you to take the streets to the north of town." Keme backed his horse up a few paces. "I'll ride south. Fire one shot in the air if you encounter anyone or anything that you deem to be a threat."

"What about Fiona?" Akule glanced back at the mule.

Dylan immediately realized what she was saying. Fiona carried the bulk of their supplies. Marathon looked deserted, but what if it wasn't? They couldn't take that risk.

"She stays with me," Keme said. "Do not enter any of the structures. Just look for..."

Keme didn't finish the sentence. It seemed to drift away in the cold winter air. Dylan thought he seemed stuck on just what they were supposed to be looking for. "Signs of life?" he suggested.

"Yeah. That. Don't take long. I want our camp set up before dark. Let's meet back here in twenty minutes."

Marathon was a small town by any standards, and the bulk of it lay to the north. Dylan rode past the fire department, the library, the high school, even out to the water supply facility. The north side of town was thirteen blocks deep and nine blocks wide. By the time he made it back to the front of the Gage, Akule and Keme were waiting for him.

"Nothing on my end," he said. "Other than burned-out homes and quite a few abandoned cars."

"Same on my end," Keme said. "Looked as if anything that could be of use to anyone has already been taken."

Akule nodded toward the two-story structure in front of them. "Hotel's deserted...unless someone's hiding inside watching us."

All three of them turned their eyes up to the second-floor windows, but they didn't see anyone staring back down at them. Not that any person hiding there would be that obvious.

"Akule, you stay here with the animals. Dylan and I will clear the rooms."

When she started to protest, he added, "You're better with the horses. Don't let them get spooked. Don't let them run."

Dylan followed Keme into the lobby. Mounted deer heads adorned the walls. The ceiling sported some kind of elaborate pressed tin crisscrossed with dark wooden beams. A western chandelier had been torn from the ceiling and left in pieces on the floor.

Keme nodded toward the hall, which led to the stairs.

They moved slowly and quietly. They cleared forty-six rooms in all.

Most had been looted, pilfered, vandalized.

But the luxury of the place peered through that destruction and stood in contrast to the world outside the windows.

King-sized beds.

Marbled bathrooms.

Glass-tiled showers.

The one thing they didn't see was people—dead or alive. It seemed to Dylan that it had been quite some time since anyone had walked these halls. He had the impression of stepping back in time to a previous generation. It hadn't been that long though. A little over six months ago, tourists were scheduling sessions at the adjacent spa, ordering cappuccinos in the coffee shop, enjoying steaks in the dining room.

Those days were gone.

Several of the rooms had snow piled inside that had drifted through the open windows. One or two had bloodstains on the floor. Anything of use had been taken.

As they made their way back to the front of the hotel, they

passed the manager's office. Dylan stepped inside and looked around. What would be of use in an office? The computers, printers, and office supplies were all worthless.

"See something?" Keme stood in the doorway, looking left, right, forward—constantly scanning.

"Just thinking that the one place looters might have overlooked..."

"Would have been an office." Keme nodded. "I'll help."

They opened drawers. Rifled through filing cabinets. Peered behind the couch. And then Dylan saw it—the thing his mind had seen and recognized. A white box on the wall with a red cross stenciled on the front. He strode over, undid the latches, and peered inside. "We've hit the motherlode."

The box was full of first aid supplies.

He dropped his pack to the floor, unzipped it, and emptied everything from the box into his pack. "I don't know how the scavengers overlooked this."

"Sometimes you don't see the things you're used to seeing. They blend into the background."

Akule was exactly where they'd left her, still sitting astride Daisy, hand on her hip holster as if she might need to draw down at any moment.

"Place is clear," Keme said. "Let's put the animals in the courtyard. We'll set up camp in the lobby."

A younger, more naïve Dylan would have protested. Why the lobby when there were forty-six rooms to choose from? He didn't ask that question because he was no longer that naïve person. Apocalypse Dylan understood they needed to stay together.

Needed to stay close to the animals.

Needed to be ready for a quick getaway.

Apocalypse Dylan understood there was no way to predict what the night might bring.

CHAPTER 5

Akule should have fallen asleep the moment she lay down. She was exhausted. Her bones hurt. How could her bones hurt when she was only twenty-two? Wasn't that an old person thing? And the weariness she felt seemed to reach to the center of her being. Thirty miles in the saddle wasn't what had worn her out. It was more the status of her soul.

Being constantly vigilant.

Trying to keep her hopes at bay while at the same time holding on to the possibility that they would find Paco and Claire and Pete and Danny. Believing it could happen, in spite of what they were and weren't seeing.

How could there be no people in Marathon?

Where had they gone?

Were they all dead?

She finally gave up on resting, slipped out of her sleeping bag, and tiptoed out of the lobby. She tossed her questions back and forth as she checked the horses. At least they provided some measure of comfort. Horses always had done that for her. They were uncomplicated. Their needs were simple. They could be counted on to be there when you needed them.

"Couldn't sleep?" Dylan stepped out of the darkness. He'd taken the first patrol. She'd heard him moving around the hotel grounds, but how had he known she was in the courtyard?

"Heard Daisy make that contented sigh horses make when you walked out here."

"Ah." She wanted to ask him if there'd been any sign of anyone, but of course the answer to that was *no*. If there had been, he would have alerted them. So instead she said, "Guess I'm kinda keyed up."

"Yeah. I get that." Dylan leaned against the adobe wall, arms crossed.

She could only make out his shadow, but she could tell from his tone that his smile was firmly intact.

Even in the low light of the Texas moon, or maybe because of it, Dylan Spencer looked as if he'd stepped off the front cover of *Team Roping*. When they'd been in high school, he'd known how handsome he was. He'd always struck her as cocky, arrogant, determined to prove something. He was still determined to prove something, but the arrogance had been chipped away by the events of June 6th and all that followed.

Anyone who was arrogant now was a fool.

As for the cockiness, it seemed tempered with something else.

Experience, she supposed.

"Remember this place?" he asked.

"Do I remember it?"

"Senior prom. A couple car loads of us came here."

"Yeah. I remember it. That seems like...ages ago."

"Another lifetime."

"Literally." She tried not to smile. She didn't want to get in the habit of smiling at Dylan Spencer, but the memory of their younger selves flooded her mind and she almost laughed. "Your date was Suzie Langford. I thought she was the silliest thing in Alpine...blonde, always made-up as if she were about to be on television, dressed like Barbie."

"Yeah. She might have been too smart for me. Ended up getting a scholarship to Yale. Last I heard she'd made it into law school and was interning during the summers for a legal team in Boston."

"Boston. I wonder what Boston's like now..." And there it was, Akule thought.

You simply couldn't get away from it.

The fact that the world had changed.

"For the life of me, I cannot remember who your date was that night."

"Justin Dodd. He had a bad habit of dipping Skoal, forgetting he had it in his mouth, and trying to kiss a girl."

"That's right. We dared him to jump in the swimming pool, and he did—fully dressed."

Akule allowed the warmth of that memory to raise her spirits for a moment, then she sobered. "He died, you know. Battle of Marfa."

"Yeah. I did know that."

"He was a good guy."

"He was."

Akule pushed away from the wall she'd been leaning against. She thought it was probably best to share her reservations up front, put them out in the open, get them off her chest. She walked over to where Dylan waited, stopped a few inches in front of him, and stuck her hands in her pockets.

"Why are you here, Dylan?"

"I was walking the perimeter, and like I said, I heard Daisy—"

"Not what I meant."

He sighed, and she was standing close enough to see the drop in his shoulders.

"I always planned to leave Alpine. Not for good. Not even for a few years like you did."

"We're not talking about me."

"I always admired the fact that you lived in Houston and Austin."

"I was homeless part of the time, sponging off friends the other part. Nothing to admire about that."

"Yeah, but you had the courage to do it. To give life somewhere else a try. You've always had the courage to do whatever you thought you should do."

She wasn't sure that courage was actually what he was referring to. She'd never thought of herself that way. She'd always felt as if she was staggering from one decision to another. But this conversation wasn't about her. Or it wasn't supposed to be. So she repeated her question.

"Why are you here, Dylan?"

"Lots of reasons, honestly. Yes, I wanted out of Alpine, and this might be my only chance."

"Meaning what?"

"Meaning that things might get worse. That we might have to hunker down even more than we already are. When I think that I might be old one day and all I experienced of life was one town..." He shook his head, his passion coloring his tone and causing his shoulders to tighten. "What if this is our only chance to see what the rest of the world looks like?"

"Okay." She drew the word out slowly. "You could have..."

"What? Gone off on my own? I'm not that stupid. I suppose I could have tried to talk someone into going with me, but then I would have been responsible if something happened to them. Huh-uh. But you were already going. You'd already made up your mind. I'm not putting you at risk, and I'm not putting your dad at risk. I'm just riding along."

"Just riding along..." She was developing an irritating habit of repeating what he said, mostly because the things he said brought her up short.

"And who knows, Akule. Maybe I'll even end up being helpful."

She laughed then—it slipped out, snuck around the guard she usually kept between herself and other people. "Maybe, Dylan. You did good finding the first aid supplies."

"You already had some."

"Nothing like what you found. That was more like a battlefield triage kit—clotting powder, sutures, painkillers. It was a real find."

"Hopefully we won't need it."

"Yeah, that would be good. Maybe it will be something we take back to Alpine as a gift, a sort of thank you for everyone's donation to the cause. I have no doubt that Cade, Miles, and Logan would be happy to add it to our emergency supplies in Alpine."

"The good doctors."

"That they are."

"You should get some sleep."

"You're right. I should." She made her way across the dark courtyard aware that Dylan was watching her.

Could she hear the laughter of the kids they used to be?

The splash Justin Dodd had made as he'd jumped into the pool?

The sound of her own crying when she learned of his death?

She thought she could hear all of those things and more. Maybe, just maybe, she could hear the whispers of her nephews as they spoke to one another. Were they huddled near a campsite or in their home or at a government refugee center?

Were they still alive?

Akule climbed into her sleeping bag that she'd spread out on the couch in the lobby. They'd opted not to have a fire until morning, not to risk drawing attention to their presence. The room was cold, and she snuggled down into the bag until only her nose and eyes weren't covered.

She should have fallen right to sleep.

But she spent another hour staring up at the ceiling tiles.

Wondering if having Dylan Spencer with them might end up being helpful or something she would regret.

Keme had taken the middle watch—the longer watch. He felt like it was his duty, as the oldest in the group. Truthfully, he'd learned to get by on much less sleep than in the old days. After his shift, he slept hard. He slept without dreaming. And he woke to the smell of campfire coffee.

Akule and Dylan were sitting in front of the small cooking fire they'd built in the lobby's fireplace, each clutching a mug and staring at him.

"What? Was I drooling?" He sat up, rubbing his hand over his face, brushing back his hair, which had come loose from its band.

"I've never seen anyone sleep that hard," Dylan admitted.

"He's always been like that." Akule stood, poured another mug of coffee, and pushed it into her father's hands. "When Paco and I were young, we used to make tiny paper wads and throw them at him."

"You and Paco were a handful. Wait until you have kids. You'll see."

Which sort of killed the early-morning, good-feeling vibe they had going. Who knew if Akule or Dylan would have children? Who knew what the next day. . . hell, what this day. . . would bring?

"Horses are fed and watered. Dylan and I were able to fetch some buckets of water and pour them into the courtyard's fountain."

"Where'd you find water?"

"Old trough next to the pump house."

"Remind me to sleep in every day." But as he stood and walked toward the broken windows, he saw that dawn was just breaking. He hadn't slept in. Akule and Dylan had woken early. Akule, he suspected, was ready to go.

The ride from Marathon to Sanderson was fifty-four miles, and Keme expected it would take a day and a half.

On Saturday they rode all day, then pitched their tents five hundred feet off the road when they stopped for the night. The stars stretched above them like a canopy. Occasionally, Keme was able to see a positive side to the new path the world had been forced on to. No more need for dark sky programs. He supposed everyone the whole world over were able to see the Milky Way as clearly as he could.

They slept undisturbed, maintained their patrol, and were riding again before the morning sun broke the horizon on Sunday morning.

The wind was from the north and cold enough to make his teeth ache. The desert stretched out uninterrupted in every direction. There wasn't a single manmade structure to be seen.

Keme knew there was a lot of wide-open space in their part of Texas. It was why people moved there. Why people stayed there. The area certainly wasn't for everyone, but people who were uncomfortable with the frenzied growth of the last fifty years found this part of Texas to be a place of refuge.

Driving through that refuge in a car was one thing.

Riding across it on the back of a horse was another.

They took a twenty-minute break around noon. Saw to their bathroom needs. Ate the same lunch they'd had the previous two days. Studied the horizon, then mounted their horses and continued east.

"Don't know much about Sanderson," Dylan confessed.

They were riding three abreast, with Fiona-the-mule lagging only a few steps behind.

"Not a lot to know." Keme shifted in his saddle. The day was bright and sunny and most of the snow had melted away. But the night would be cold, as the previous night had been. He was hoping they could find a place to camp indoors when they reached Sanderson.

"The Coen brothers filmed *No Country for Old Men* there."

"No shit?" Dylan looked at Akule as if she was trying to pull one over on him.

"She's right. I'd forgotten about that. There's a train station and an airport."

"How many people?"

"Less than seven hundred, if I remember right."

"The question is whether anyone is still there." Akule leaned forward to pat Daisy on the neck.

Dylan turned in the saddle to frown at Akule and her mare. "That beast has already tried to nip me twice today."

"Not Daisy. Maybe you're thinking of a different horse."

"I'm thinking that she doesn't like me."

"Huh. Got any peppermints? She's very fond of peppermints."

"How do you know that? When did you have peppermints?"

"Not that long ago."

"Where'd you get them?"

"Can't say."

"You have a supplier."

"Had. He ran out months ago."

Keme stopped his horse. Dylan and Akule followed suit.

"What did you see?" Akule put a hand over her eyes, trying to block the glare of the desert sun.

"Reflection...that way." Keme nodded east, toward Sanderson.

Dylan reached for his binoculars. "Think they have a patrol?"

"I think we're about to find out."

They had a plan for this. They'd talked it through several times. Keme would approach on foot. Akule and Dylan would hang back. Wait with the animals. Watch the scene unfold through the binoculars. Keme would whistle if things seemed on the up and up. If they weren't...

If they weren't, that would be obvious pretty fast.

They approached slowly, stopping occasionally to carefully glass the area. Three men stood in the middle of the road. They appeared to be armed.

"Here goes." Keme dismounted and handed Amber's lead rope to Akule.

"Be careful, Dad."

"Yeah, Mr. Lopez. Don't take any chances."

But they all knew that life was a chance. Getting up that morning was a chance. Heading east, heading farther away from home, was definitely a chance.

Five minutes later he could make out that the three men in the middle of the road were older, probably ranchers by the way they stood and the way they clutched their rifles. Standing beside each man was a large dog.

Keme stopped when he was close enough that the men could hear him. Not too close though. He'd intentionally stayed back far enough that he didn't have a chance of being hit by a bullet. He stopped, held his hands out wide, and shouted, "We'd like to pass through."

"How many of you are there?"

This was one of those details they hadn't been able to agree on. Keme was for saying he was alone, but then that would soon be proven to be a lie. Dylan wanted him to say there were over twenty behind him—a show of force. Akule wanted him to simply state the truth.

He chose not to answer the question.

"We'll keep going if you'd rather we don't stop in your town. But we'd like to go through. Around is..." He glanced out at the desert. "Harder."

He again saw the reflection of sunlight off glass.

Someone in the group was using binoculars. If Akule and Dylan could clearly see the Sanderson Welcome Committee, then the three men standing in front of him could also clearly see them.

The three appeared to confer, and then the rancher in the middle shouted, "You can pass. Don't try anything funny though. My friend will put a bullet in the center of your head faster than you can reach for that pistol."

Keme had no doubt the old guy was telling the truth. West Texas ranchers were serious about their firearms and notorious for their skill with said firearms.

Keme continued to hold his arms out at his side.

See? Nothing to worry about here.

"I'm going to signal my daughter and her friend that it's okay to come on."

"Go ahead. But remember, no...."

"Funny stuff. Got it." This Keme muttered to himself, then he turned and whistled once.

Akule and Dylan were at his side in under two minutes. He

hoisted himself into the saddle, and they moved forward. When they were still ten yards out—close enough to see better, far enough away that they could still make a run for it —they again stopped.

"My name is Keme Lopez. We're traveling from Alpine to Dallas."

The three men again consulted each other, then the one in the middle...the one that had been carrying on the negotiations and reminded Keme of Tommy Lee Jones in that old movie Akule had mentioned...raised a hand and said, "Come on through, son. It sounds like your journey is just beginning."

CHAPTER 6

Dylan had spent a good hour poring over the maps before they left Alpine, studying Keme's route, looking for weaknesses or worrisome spots.

Sanderson was located at the juncture of US 90E and US Hwy 285 S. It was a good eighty-five miles south of Fort Stockton, which they'd been intent on avoiding. But they had to turn north eventually to reach the Dallas metroplex. Keme's plan had been to turn north at Dryden, cross I-10 at Sheffield, and then meander north and east toward San Angelo. At that point they'd be halfway there.

Spending the night in Sanderson made sense, and they might be able to find out what they were heading into.

The three old guys had lead them back to their home—a Texas ranch house if there ever was one. It was set on the north side of town and tucked into a bend midway up a large hill. The home was designed in an L shape. A five-foot-high brick wall turned that shape into a U and shielded the light of their campfire from any curious eyes. The open end of the U faced the desert to the west.

Was anyone out there?

Was anyone watching?

The three old guys were joined by two old women. It amazed Dylan that these people had made it through the last six months. He still thought surviving took youth, energy, and the ability to change. But he was beginning to question those beliefs.

They were eating outside even though it was cold.

The wind had died so that inside the house and outside in the courtyard were nearly the same temperature—hovering a few degrees above freezing, according to the thermometer near the back door. Stella explained that it helped her faith to eat under the stars. Dylan had no idea what that meant, but since they'd been allowed to feed, water, and stable their mares and the mule Fiona, he wasn't about to argue with her.

They'd already discussed the cause of the June 6th cataclysm—certainly something to do with satellites though the jury was out as to whether it was terrorism, an act of war, or a natural event.

He finished off his second bowl of stew and wiped his mouth with the back of his hand. "Thank you, ma'am. That was very good."

"Nice to have a young man to appreciate my cooking." She scraped what was left in the bottom of the stew pot into three dog bowls and placed it in front of three German shepherds that waited for a nod from her before lapping it up.

Stella Bright looked to be in her eighties. She reminded Dylan of a librarian at Alpine High who had looked past the kid who had thrown away his sophomore year to the kid that just might have learned his lesson. She looked kind.

Jimbo Bright sat back with a sigh. "Been married to this woman for sixty years, and never regretted it a day. She can cook, sew, and shoot straight."

Lester Davis nodded in agreement. "She's our secret weapon."

Stella shushed them, donned two oven mitts, and pulled the Dutch oven full of blackberry cobbler from the fire. "We'd been planning on a special dessert, since it's New Year's Eve and all."

Dylan blinked twice, looked around the circle, and shook his head. "I forgot about that."

"It's not like anyone is going to set off fireworks," Jimbo said.

"No watching the ball drop in Times Square." Lester looked up at the stars. "Wouldn't want to be in New York City right now."

Which, to Dylan, was a pretty sobering thought. Had New York, Los Angeles, or Chicago survived? What would living in any city be like? Surely there had to be at least one place across this vast country where people had figured out how to turn the lights back on.

Stella pulled the lid off the cobbler and smiled. "We'll celebrate without the television tonight. We'll celebrate like you're supposed to—with your loved ones and your friends. Dorothy, want to gather up their bowls for me?"

Dorothy was probably the youngest of the group. Dylan guessed she was in her sixties. She was the younger sister of Lester.

Nathan rounded out the group. He was tall and leathery with a gaze that seemed to miss nothing.

Keme accepted the bowl of cobbler with a nod and thanks.

Dylan hadn't eaten anything sweet in months. With the first bite of cobbler, he closed his eyes and groaned. Everyone laughed.

"Lester has a few beehives," Stella explained.

"And the berries?" Akule held up a spoonful and stared at it as if she couldn't quite believe her eyes.

"You just have to know where they are and be there when they're ready to pick."

"Stella once taught home economics at the high school. She loves to can fruits, vegetables, even meats. Good thing, as I didn't know anything about it." Dorothy glanced up at her friend and smiled. "But I'm learning."

"How did the five of you come to be here alone?"

Jimbo answered Keme's questions. "Stella and I grew up here. Never felt a need to leave. Lester, he's a newcomer."

"Yup. Moved to town ten years ago. In West Texas time, that makes you the new kid on the block. Course Nathan's been here less time than me, so now he's the new kid."

"I was on the Dryden City Council," Nathan said. "When the council fell—when we were replaced by the goons in charge now—I headed west."

"Didn't make it far, my friend." Jimbo nodded his head appreciatively. "And we're grateful you joined what's left of Sanderson."

Lester had passed on the cobbler, explaining that he was borderline diabetic. "I bought the pharmacy here ten years ago, when the previous owner got tired of low profits and dealing with insurance. When Nathan arrived...I guess that was around June 16th..."

"Ten days after the event." Firelight reflected off of Dorothy's glasses. "It all fell so quickly."

"When Nathan arrived and told us how terrible things were in Dryden, Jimbo went back with me to convince my sister to move."

"Didn't take much convincing," Dorothy said. "I was the accountant for nearly every business in Dryden, but no one needed an accountant after June 6th. I only wish some of my neighbors, my friends, would have come as well."

"We tried, but people weren't easily convinced in those early days."

"Where did everyone else from Sanderson go?" Akule asked.

She was staring longingly into her empty cobbler bowl. Dylan had the funny image of her licking it like he was tempted to do. Instead, she set it aside with an appreciative look and a nod at Stella.

"I guess you know how it was." Jimbo ran a hand over the top of his head. His hair was thinning. His skin, thin and spotted. "Some went toward the cities, hoping it was merely a technological glitch out here in the desert."

"Do you think that's true?" Dylan felt hope rise in spite of himself.

"No. I don't. In fact, we've been told just the opposite since. Most of the traffic we see now is headed away from the cities. Some people are even headed to Mexico, thinking things might be better there. You're the first people we've seen going east and north in some time."

"What about the people who didn't head to the cities?" Keme sat forward. "Where is everyone?"

"Some died." Jimbo shook his head. "We had a lot of that the first few weeks. Some went to the larger towns like Dryden."

"That was a mistake," Nathan said. "The people who replaced the duly elected city council were thugs. Course, they were able to do that because the council was slow to act. People were frightened. Strength—any strength—seemed better than indecision."

"What specifically did the new leaders do?" Keme glanced

at his daughter and then at Dylan. "Anything you can tell us will help since we plan on going through there."

Nathan was frowning and shaking his head before Keme finished talking. "I gotta be honest with you. I wouldn't do that. The first thing they did was shut down the road going through town and implement a *tax*."

"A tax?" Akule had befriended one of the dogs and was running her hand over its head, massaging its ears.

That dog looked to Dylan like it could swallow her hand in one bite. But it wouldn't. It was looking at her with pure devotion.

"They called it a tax. Those people didn't act like government representatives though. They acted more like trolls guarding a bridge. Initially it was small things they'd insist you give them—*a fair trade for passage through* is how they explained it. As resources have become more scarce their methods became even more cruel. The last people that came through were headed to Mexico. They were forced to give up both of their firearms, all of their bullets, and all of their food." Anger swept across his face. "No way those people would have made it to the border and across with what supplies they had left after they got through Dryden. They had nothing except the clothes they were wearing and the old nags they were riding."

"What did they do?"

"Stayed here a few weeks. Collected water with the rains. We couldn't spare much food, but they were able to hunt with a slingshot the kid had and put back some meat. I sure hope they made it."

Keme nodded in understanding. "We had something similar happen with our surrounding towns. Fort Davis set up a barricade, which my sister was able to negotiate her way through. That's how we learned about the satellites. She and a few others went up to the observatory and talked to the scientists working there."

"Wait...your sister is Tanda Lopez?" Jimbo's eyes widened.

All of the Sanderson group leaned forward as if they were afraid of missing Keme's answer.

"Yeah. She was the police chief in Alpine. Still is."

"She's a legend," Stella said.

"We've heard all about her." Dorothy looked at her brother, who nodded in agreement.

Nathan added, "Heard she ousted the old mayor who was crooked."

Keme shifted in his chair. "Well, yes, but..."

"And battled with Marfa when they tried to steal all your supplies."

"We all battled with Marfa," Dylan corrected. "But Tanda, she led us."

"And fought the Watchmen."

"My aunt wasn't about to let those people terrorize our town or any people trying to come to our town." Akule crossed her arms. "Tanda thinks law and order still exist. . . or at least she thinks they should."

There was a moment of silence, then Jimbo said almost reverently, "She sounds like one of the good ones."

"She is. She definitely is. She wanted to come with us, but she wouldn't leave Alpine. The winter months have been hard on everyone, and then there's my parents..." Keme appeared lost in that thought for a moment.

Which of course reminded Dylan of his mother.

He hadn't expected to find himself worrying about her, but he did. She wasn't really alone, as she'd suggested to Keme, but he understood that she felt that way sometimes.

Keme held his hands toward the fire. "We can't go back the

way we came. It would take too long, and we want to avoid Fort Stockton at all costs."

"You're correct on that point. Heard there are bodies hanging in the streets there." Nathan steepled his fingers together. "Was your plan to turn north on 349 and cross Interstate 10 at Sheffield?"

"Yes."

Nathan looked to the other four in his group who all nodded. "We might have a better way. It's not exactly public roads, but it'll get you north of Dryden. I'll draw you a map."

Coming from anyone else, Dylan wouldn't have wanted to risk it. They were heading across the desert.

It could be a trap.

It could be a death trap.

But he knew that in this world you had to be willing to trust the good guys. These people were on the right side of things. Nathan was adamant about the alternate route, and his way—if it worked—allowed them to cross I-10 on a county road to the east of Sheffield.

Keme didn't look completely convinced. "Have you been this way yourself?"

"Nope. Not since June 6th, but it'll get you where you want to go. And it'll get you there in one piece, which won't be the case if you go through Dryden."

Akule reached forward and traced the route Lester had drawn on a clean sheet of paper. Dylan wondered how many sheets of paper were left in the world, then pushed that thought out of his mind.

What difference did it make?

They had what they needed now.

"Dryden won't have patrols out this far?" She tapped the spot where Lester's map came closest to Dryden—a fair distance, but was it a safe distance?

"Can't say for certain." Lester looked to Dorothy and Stella, Jimbo and Nathan.

It was Dorothy who answered. "My guess would be they're too lazy to patrol out that far. And what's the point? No one's out there. These people who are in control of the town aren't virtuous. They're not hard workers or big thinkers. They're thugs, plain and simple."

Keme turned to Akule and asked, "Do we go with Lester's map or stick to our original plan?"

"Lester's map." She didn't even hesitate.

Then he turned to Dylan. "Do you agree?"

And in the next moment, Dylan's respect for Keme went up —something he wouldn't have thought was possible. Because in that moment Dylan saw that Keme didn't think he had all the answers. He needed the advice and counsel of other people he knew and trusted, even if it was his daughter and a kid from his hometown.

"I think Nathan's way makes sense."

Keme nodded in agreement, and Dylan accepted they weren't just allowing him to tag along. They were a solid group of three and what decisions needed to be made would be made together.

They'd learned the importance of that in Alpine.

They'd learned the importance of that from Tanda.

Keme stood and shook Lester's hand. "We'll leave at first light."

THE GROUP BROKE up soon after that. Akule's father and Dylan went to check on the horses. Lester, Nathan, and Jimbo walked with them.

Akule helped Stella carry the dishes inside. Dorothy made

sure the dogs had plenty of water. The animals slept outside and maintained a perimeter guard that Jimbo swore was better than any man could do.

"I hope you find your brother." Stella stacked the dishes and then tied an apron around her waist.

It was such a simple, everyday gesture.

Or, it had been.

The only person that Akule had ever known to wear an apron was her grandmother. She supposed in the old days it was important to protect your clothes. Throwing a load of soiled laundry in the washing machine had become something Akule's generation had taken for granted.

Something else they'd taken for granted.

A gas lantern on the kitchen counter provided a soft glow. Dorothy brought in a kettle of water that had been heated on the fire. After placing it on the stove, she squeezed Stella's arm and smiled at Akule.

It seemed to Akule that Dorothy's smile had to push past some unspoken pain. The woman was making a valiant effort to look as if all was well, but it obviously wasn't.

"If you two have this covered, I think I'll go on to bed."

"Of course, Dorothy. Sleep well, my friend."

When she'd left the room, Akule asked, "Is she okay?"

"Most days she is. Dorothy has advanced osteoarthritis. The medication she was taking before June 6th helped ease the pain, but that ran out months ago." She squirted the smallest amount of soap in the sink, added the hot water, and slipped in the first dish. "Now we're trying what herbs we can grow."

"Is that working?"

"Some days it works better than others."

"Life is so hard." Akule picked up a bowl from the rinse water and dried it with a dishtowel that was old and soft and nearly transparent.

"Life is hard, but God is good."

At Stella's words, she froze. Akule studied the woman and wondered if she really believed what she'd just said. Finally she sighed, finished drying the bowl, and placed it in the cabinet. "I'm not so sure."

"If God is good?"

"Just look around, Stella. This is good?"

Stella leaned toward the window over the sink and peered out into the darkness. "Look at those stars, Akule. Look around you. You're traveling with your father and your friend. I know you're grateful for them. I can tell by the way you look at them that they mean a lot to you."

"Yeah. They do." She realized even Dylan meant a lot to her, and that came as a surprise. "They do. Still, I'm not sure I believe in God anymore. Everything that's happened has struck me as so random, so pointless."

"It does seem that way at times."

"But you think..." Akule couldn't find the words.

Her mind stopped at the mention of belief of any kind. She'd given up on that long ago, even before June 6th. She'd given up on that when she was sleeping on a bench in Austin—though she now understood that her homelessness then had been mostly her own doing.

Still, where had God been when she hadn't known which direction to turn? She had prayed. She'd cried out to God, and she hadn't heard a thing in response.

Where was God then?

Where was God when the people of Marfa attacked Alpine?

Why did he allow people like the Watchmen to exist?

But those things weren't what she said. Instead, she spoke of the wound in her heart that still ached. The wound that remained fresh and raw and painful. "My mother died...she was killed actually, defending Alpine."

Stella let the bowl she was washing sink into the dishwater. She wiped her hands on her apron, turned to Akule, and put a hand on each of her shoulders. "I am truly sorry for your loss."

They weren't just hollow words. She quite obviously meant what she said. Her expression filled with compassion. Tears shone in her eyes. Her voice was husky when she repeated, "I am truly, truly sorry."

Akule nodded, then allowed this woman she'd known only a few hours to pull her into a hug.

When they stepped apart, Stella laughed lightly. "That's one change in me since June 6th...I tear up more easily. But I think I laugh more easily too."

"Why is that?"

"I don't know. It feels like I'm more tender toward life. Everything seems precious and holy, even our pain."

Akule had no idea what that meant.

"The connection between a daughter and a mother is a strong one, the first connection we experience. My mother died of cancer fourteen years ago, and I still feel that loss every day."

"But you believe God is good."

"I do." She didn't defend herself. She didn't try to preach to Akule. Instead she smiled softly and began scrubbing the pot the cobbler had been cooked in.

Akule honestly didn't know what she believed.

She was usually too tired to consider faith or goodness.

Some nights, though, she did struggle with the *why* of things. Those were nights when she was so tired she wanted to weep and yet she couldn't sleep. She would sit at the small kitchenette table in her apartment, and try as she might, she couldn't make head or tails of the world she was caught up in.

Why had June 6th happened?

Would their life ever return to normal?

How would Alpine survive another attack?

What would she do if she lost her father?

Standing in Stella's kitchen, she still didn't have answers to those questions, but she was grateful that they'd stopped in Sanderson. Glad they'd met these people. Not only had the evening provided a much-needed respite, but visiting with this small group had better equipped them for their journey.

She understood that this was an evening she would remember long into old age, if she lived to an old age. Having spent an evening with Stella and Jimbo, Lester and Dorothy, had enriched her life. Akule didn't know what lay ahead. She didn't know whether she'd find Paco or how long it would take to return home.

She didn't know if God was good.

But at least she knew there were still some good people in the world.

For the moment, that was enough.

CHAPTER 7

Nathan's route proved to be a good one.

They saw no more burned-out cars.

Came across no desiccated bodies.

The homes and farms they saw at a distance appeared to be abandoned. Had the people left? Had they died? Keme was tempted to stop and search the homes for supplies, but he was also anxious to keep moving. So they didn't stop. They passed, staring at the farmsteads from a distance and wondering about the people who had once lived there, farmed the land, married and raised children and watched sunsets.

"Feels like we're the only people left in the world," Akule said.

Dylan held his hand over his heart. "We're it? You just trashed my dreams, woman. I was hoping we'd see some golden arches. I could do with a Quarter Pounder, fries, and a shake right now."

"Did you have to bring up fast food?"

"Might as well share my daydreams."

"You're killin' me, Smalls."

"Yup. I'm killing myself too."

There was no evidence at all that anyone had recently traveled this way. That might have been because they were following caliche county roads. The white rock made for a rough ride. Weeds had grown up, completely obscuring it in places. From a distance, it wouldn't even look like a road, and since GPS didn't work anymore perhaps the county road had been forgotten.

The horses didn't mind. Much of the way, they were able to ride on the edge of fields that paralleled the road. When Keme called for stops, when they each climbed down to walk and stretch, the horses were able to graze on scraggly winter grass.

Nathan had even marked natural springs where they could water the horses.

Keme had originally figured 200 miles from Dryden to the spot marked on Franklin Kurtz's envelope. He had calculated that would take seven days. Going Nathan's way, they approached the outskirts of San Angelo nine days after leaving Sanderson and twelve days after leaving Alpine. Nearly two weeks and they were only halfway to Dallas.

"Sure feels like a roundabout way to get to Dallas," Akule said.

"Because it is." Keme shrugged. "How fast we get there isn't as important as knowing what we're heading into. Our chances of success go up with every piece of information we're given."

"I guess."

On the positive side, the weather had cooperated.

"Feels like my butt has taken on the form of this saddle." Dylan reached forward and patted Texas Lady's neck.

"It's amazing what you can get used to." Akule pulled down on her ball cap to shield her eyes from the morning sun. "Sleeping on the ground is starting to feel normal."

They were tired though. Keme could feel weariness creeping into his bones. They needed a night off the ground. Needed real food, not dried jerky. Needed to see some light at the end of the tunnel.

Outside of San Angelo, all the homes they passed looked abandoned. Some had been burned. Others had been looted. They didn't see people until they crossed Highway 67. There was activity in a neighborhood east of Farm to Market Road 2288.

They could see people outside—fetching water from containers that had been positioned to catch the snow, checking on plants in greenhouses, and playing with children.

No one raised a hand in greeting.

No one acknowledged their presence.

Keme nodded toward a barricade positioned across the entrance to the subdivision. They dismounted, then slowly—in a nonthreatening way—walked their horses over to three teens who leaned against the back of the truck, each cradling a rifle.

"Don't come any closer, mister."

Keme felt more than saw Akule and Dylan stop beside him.

"We're just passing through."

"That's what everyone says until they try to rob you." This from a skinny kid who couldn't have been more than fourteen.

"Or kill you." A girl with long hair tied in braids passed her rifle from her right hand to her left and back again. She was comfortable with it. She wanted them to know she felt at ease with the firearm.

Keme didn't doubt for a minute that she was efficient with it too.

"Only thing we want is information."

Finally the leader of the group spoke—a young man who should have been sitting in a high school biology class or working out in the weight room preparing for summer sports. "That ain't free. . . not anymore."

"All right. I understand."

They'd discussed this around their campfire earlier that morning. It was important to know what they were riding into. They were willing to pay, but they had to be judicious about how they used the things they had to trade.

Akule retrieved a pack of cigarettes from her backpack and passed it to her father.

"I'm sure you three don't smoke, but maybe you know someone who could use these." Keme walked his horse closer, but not too close.

When the older boy nodded, he tossed the pack to him.

"Those things will kill you," Dylan said.

"Ain't gonna smoke them, but we'll trade them. Some people have no more sense than they did before June 6th. They'll trade food for smokes." He passed the cigarettes to the other boy, who put them in a backpack.

That confirmed Keme's assumption that the girl was the best shot of the three. She kept her hands on her rifle. Kept her eyes pinned on them.

"What information do you want?"

Keme nodded east. "San Angelo?"

"Most of downtown burned. Don't ask me why. Never made sense to me to set something on fire that you might need later, but then you passed the grocery store so you know it's par for the course."

"Can we expect safe passage around town?"

"You cannot."

"Because..."

"Because most of this town is split into three gangs. None of them care for strangers."

"Okay." The next question—the only question that really

mattered—was one he had to ask carefully. He didn't want to give away the location of Franklin's family, but he needed to know what they were riding into.

"Thought we'd skirt the state park, then head north. What can we expect from that direction?"

"Same thing you can expect from any direction—trouble. In case you haven't noticed, people aren't too friendly anymore."

"Right." He glanced at Akule who shrugged.

Dylan muttered, "Not sure that was worth a single cigarette, let alone a pack."

"All right," Keme said. "Thank you for the information."

They each turned their horses. Keme touched his heels lightly to his mare's side, and as he did the girl spoke up. "There's some family groups around Fisher Lake. Some are mean, but most are just hunkered down, trying to survive the winter."

Keme nodded as if that made sense.

"And there's a survivalist group—north and west of the park. You'll want to avoid them."

"Why's that?"

"Because they'd as soon shoot you as have you pass through their land. In fact, you can't pass through their land. They're not friendly like us."

"If you stay on 2288 you'll be okay," the older boy added. "Just don't wander off on the west side. Not until you're well past the lake."

The problem with that suggestion was that Franklin's map directed them to a spot west of 2288—exactly where the girl was warning them not to go.

Keme waited until they were out of sight of the teens and their neighborhood, then he pulled his mare to a stop.

"Ideas?"

"We came all this way." Akule frowned at nothing in particular. "According to Franklin's map, we have to go right by the place those punks told us to avoid."

"Sounds to me like it *is* the place they told us to avoid." Dylan sighed. "How about I go first and check it out?"

"No." Akule and Keme said the word at the same time with the same forcefulness.

Keme smiled at his daughter and they high-fived.

"Fine." Dylan held up both hands in surrender. "Just a suggestion."

"First of all, are we sure we want to do this?" Akule fidgeted in her saddle. "Are we sure they can tell us anything that will be helpful?"

"No," Keme admitted. "But being this close, I'd really like to see Franklin. He was always a stand-up guy. He'll help us if he can, even if it only means giving us information about what we're facing."

Which seemed to settle the question.

"We don't want to sneak up on them," Keme added. "That could be misinterpreted. We approach in an obvious and open way. Maybe they won't shoot us."

It seemed like a plan.

Seemed like the practical thing to do.

They rode single file, in order to look less threatening.

Their firearms were holstered.

They made no attempt to move silently.

According to Franklin's map, they were to turn left on a county road adjacent to the north end of the lake, then right onto a private road.

They missed the private road on their first pass, rode another half a mile, then turned around to search for it again. There it was—grown over as if no one had been in or out in a very long time.

Or maybe it was just made to look that way.

They turned the horses onto the dirt lane, rode maybe a hundred yards, and stopped in front of a large piece of plyboard that had been mounted on a metal frame and placed across the road. The paint was faded and vines had grown up and over the frame, obscuring much of the rusted metal. The thing was ridiculously huge. It took up most of the road, and they could only go around it if they got off their horses and led them.

Painted in large red letters were the words—

Stop and turn back
Trespassers will be shot

"Short and to the point," Akule said.

"Why does everyone have such a bad attitude?" Dylan rubbed at the back of his neck. "Why can't we all just get along?"

"Let's keep going." Keme dismounted and led his mare forward.

Dylan did the same, springing back up into the saddle once he was past the sign and taking the front position.

Akule came through next, leading her mare and the pack mule. When she climbed into the saddle, Daisy tossed her head as if to say, "Let's get on with this."

Keme took the rearguard.

If someone attacked, he hoped they would attack from the back. He hoped to be the first line of defense.

The lane was uncomfortably narrow.

Studying it, Keme realized it had been made that way purposely. Old farm equipment had been dumped to the right and left. The path that remained might have once been wide enough for a car, but it wasn't any longer. The brush on both sides had grown tall and Kudzu vine covered the fence line and the equipment, reshaping useless power poles and scraggy trees into something from a horror flick.

It was midday, but the sun had slipped behind the clouds.

A chill crept along Keme's spine.

Something was very wrong here.

He had the unmistakable impression that they had stepped into a trap. They could go back, but turning the horses would be difficult. Going to the left or right would be impossible. Forward was now the only direction.

They'd barely gone another fifty feet when he heard the unmistakable click a revolver made when the hammer was pulled back.

"Stop right there." The person sounded as if he were directly behind Keme. The defense, if that's what this was, had come from the direction Keme had expected it to come from. So far, no surprises.

Then, another man on horseback rode his mount out in front of Akule.

Keme glanced behind him.

Two men sat atop two horses. Both holding their pistols —cocked.

They couldn't go left, right, backward or forward.

No way out.

The man in the front stared at them without speaking.

From behind him, Keme heard, "Another group that can't read."

"Maybe they thought we were kidding."

"We weren't kidding."

Keme raised his hands. "I'm sorry. We saw the sign, but—"

"Your mistake, buddy." The man in the front raised his

voice only a fraction, but it was enough. Keme could clearly hear him and see that he, too, was armed.

"Should have turned around while you had the chance." The man's voice was steely, resolute, cold.

"Right. I get that, but see—"

"Don't need to hear it. Don't *want* to hear it."

"If I could just show you..."

Another hammer was cocked before Keme's hand reached his pocket. "I wouldn't," the same guy who had spoken before warned.

"It's a map," Akule shouted. "He's trying to show you a map."

"We don't need a map, sweetheart. We know where we are."

"But this map was drawn by his neighbor."

"Franklin," Keme explained. "Franklin Kurtz. He lived next door to me in San Angelo and he..."

"Stop talking."

The guy in front pulled a handheld radio from his jacket pocket. "Party of three. Says they know Franklin."

Keme could hear a response, but he couldn't make out the words.

How did they have radios?

How did the radios still work?

"Got it." Lead guy returned the radio to his pocket and backed his horse onto the slightest of side trails that Keme probably wouldn't have noticed if he'd passed it. "Single file. No suspicious moves."

Another asshole rode his horse out from a path on the right. He scowled at them and muttered, "Follow me."

Dylan went first. The fact that he'd been completely silent worried Keme. Hopefully Dylan wouldn't try anything stupid. Surely, he knew that any move would be a bad move.

Akule rode in the middle, leading Fiona.

Keme brought up the rear.

Forward was the only option, but the lead rider was purposely moving slowly. The two men behind Keme pushed him so that he was too close to Fiona, who tossed her head in warning that he should back off.

But he couldn't give the mule any space.

Realizing Fiona was growing increasingly anxious, Akule tapped her heels lightly on Daisy's side. Daisy, in her usual foul-tempered mood, bolted forward and nipped Dylan's horse. Texas Lady attempted to get out of the way, but she couldn't move left or right. She couldn't move forward or back. She tossed her head and tried to rear as Daisy continued to crowd her.

Dylan leaned forward—probably to pat the mare's neck, to tell her all was fine.

He never had the chance.

As Dylan leaned forward, the guy with the radio burst through the brush. He charged onto the lane, crowding Dylan's horse even more, pushing it into the brush on the right. He might have thought Dylan was going for a weapon. Or maybe he just had the urge to hurt someone. He palmed his revolver and used his significant strength to bash it against the back of Dylan's head.

Dylan hunched forward, then slid out of the saddle and collapsed on the ground—blood pouring from the wound, his eyes closed, his breathing ragged.

And after that, things got even worse.

CHAPTER 8

Akule worked to reign in her mare, who seemed intent on stomping on Dylan's still form. Daisy reared, whinnied, and fought the bit. Akule focused on calming the mare, on dancing it back and away from Dylan. She didn't know what her dad was doing, but it couldn't be good because all of Franklin's friends seemed to be shouting and pointing their weapons.

As for Dylan, he didn't move.

Didn't look at her.

Didn't make a funny joke.

She dismounted and worked to calm her horse as the guy in charge shouted at her.

"Get back on your horse, ma'am. I will shoot."

"Shoot her, and I shoot you." That was her dad.

"You'll be dead before you can pull the trigger."

"Don't bet your life on it."

The man who had been in the lead was still crowding Texas Lady.

Akule was angry enough and scared enough to lose all sense of what she should be doing. "Back off unless you want to be scraping bodies and horses off your lane." She was surprised when he backed up. It allowed her to pull firmly on Daisy's lead, calm her, and tie her lead rope to the branches of a pecan tree.

She didn't look around.

But she was aware everyone else was still on their horses.

Everyone else was still shouting and brandishing their weapons and threatening her father.

And her father, sitting tall in his saddle and holding the old Colt 45 that belonged to his father, had never made her more proud. This might be the end of the line, but they wouldn't go cowering and begging for mercy. She felt absurdly ready for the fight.

She grabbed Texas Lady's lead rope and marched forward, giving the mare space from Daisy. The man on the horse holding what looked like a Glock walked his horse back a few more steps while he continued to shout at her.

Akule didn't bother answering.

She tied Lady's lead rope to the limb of a scraggly mesquite on the lefthand side of the lane. The horse sighed in appreciation, bobbing its head and nudging through the weeds in search of anything to eat.

Still ignoring the argument swirling around her, Akule hurried back to Dylan and dropped to the ground beside him.

"His pulse is weak," she informed her dad.

That seemed to shut up Franklin's friends, something she was inordinately grateful for. She was trying to think what Cade would do. Trying to remember her triage training.

She raised his head just enough to slip her hand under and evaluate the bleeding. "I need to apply pressure to this wound."

Keme dismounted, holstered his weapon, walked over to Akule, and knelt down beside her. He dropped his backpack on the ground and unzipped it—which caused the thugs to start up again with the shouts and warnings and waving of revolvers.

"These people are awfully trigger-happy," she murmured.

"Yeah, but they haven't shot yet."

"Don't tempt us, mister."

Keme reached into the pack and pulled out the medical kit they'd brought from Alpine.

"Not yet. I want to clean it first. Do you have a t-shirt or cloth?"

"Yeah." He pushed a clean bandana into her hand.

She again carefully raised Dylan's head, pressed the cloth to the back and felt his blood soak through.

"Is it as bad as it looks?"

"Head wounds bleed profusely."

"If they killed him—"

"If he's dead, it's your fault." Radio guy had dismounted and joined them. "You should've heeded the sign."

She wondered how her dad would answer.

She suspected he was ready to punch the guy.

She was ready to punch him.

But neither of those things happened. Instead, there was the surprising sound of a four-wheeler, and then Franklin burst through the tree line.

"Keme, I can't believe you're here." He looked from Keme to Akule to Dylan and finally turned off the four-wheeler, hurried over to where they huddled around Dylan, and crouched on the ground beside them. "What happened?"

"Horse spooked, then your goon bashed him in the head with a pistol."

"Let's get him in the Gator."

Akule and Keme loaded him into the back, with Franklin helping.

"I'm taking him to the lodge," Franklin said. Then speaking to the other men, "See if you can get my friends there without killing anyone."

If they felt reprimanded, it didn't show.

Instead, to Akule, they seemed rather smug.

They moved more quickly now—Akule leading Fiona, Keme leading Texas Lady. After fifteen minutes, the lane dumped them out on a mesa at the top of a small rise, at what looked like a compound.

They pulled their horses up to a pasture fence across from what looked like the main house of the place.

"I'll stay with the horses," Keme said. "You go."

Two of the tough guys were helping Franklin move Dylan.

Akule wanted her father with her, but she knew they couldn't risk leaving the horses unguarded, let alone all of their supplies. She nodded once, retrieved the emergency aid kit, and jogged into the house.

Franklin led her to a screened-in porch with a fire burning in a clay chiminea that was vented out through a hole in the exterior wall just above a window. Surprisingly, the chiminea managed to warm the room. A small, older woman was rocking in a chair next to a window. She glanced up at them. Didn't seem surprised. Didn't seem interested. Instead of speaking, she resumed rocking and staring out the window.

"Let's put him on the couch," Franklin said.

Brightly colored pillows decorated the wicker couch. Akule's brain wanted to snag on the strangeness of it all.

Dylan on a wicker couch.

Pillows decorated with red geraniums.

A warm sunroom.

Dylan—unconscious and bleeding.

She hadn't wanted him to come on this trip. She hadn't

wanted to let him close. Certainly hadn't wanted to care for him as a friend. But he had and he was and she did.

A tall woman wearing jeans and a sweater pushed a pile of rags into her hand and set an empty bucket next to the couch. "Try not to get blood on anything."

Which seemed like a pretty cold thing to say.

Then again, it wasn't as if you could get the upholstery cleaned.

With barely a glance at Dylan, she turned to the older woman and said, "Come on, Mom. It's time for your lunch."

The older woman allowed herself to be led out of the room.

Akule removed her dad's bandana and replaced it with one of the rags folded into a four-by-four square.

"I need to prop him up."

Franklin helped. "I can't believe this happened. I can't believe you're here."

Placing two additional rags between his head and the couch, Akule reached for Dylan's hand, pressed her fingertips against his wrist, and counted.

That was when he opened his eyes.

He didn't look at the ceiling or mention the ridiculous pillows or comment on the fire in the chiminea. He took no notice of Franklin. He looked straight into Akule's eyes. "Hey. You're holding my hand."

"I'm checking your pulse."

"Yeah, but...you're holding my hand."

"I'm holding your wrist. You have a head injury."

"What happened?"

"A goon hit you with his pistol."

"Oh." He reached for the back of his head, but she stopped him.

"The bleeding is beginning to slow."

"So, it didn't kill me?"

"I suspect your head is much harder than that."

She hadn't known how frightened she was until that split second when he smiled at her. She didn't want Dylan to die. She didn't want to tell his mother that he wasn't coming home. And she was self-aware enough to admit to herself that she had grown accustomed to having him around.

Glancing at Franklin, who was still hovering nearby, Akule said, "Friendly people you have around here."

"I know." He cleared his throat. "Are you okay by yourself here?"

Her eyebrows arched. As if there were imminent danger on the screened-in porch. But maybe there was. Sometimes danger came from the most unlikely places. She felt for her pistol, reassured herself that she could defend herself and Dylan.

"Yeah. We're good."

"I'll go talk to your dad." He stood, put another small log in the chiminea, and then he was gone.

"My head hurts."

"I suspect it does. Any nausea?"

"A little."

"How many fingers do you see?"

"Six."

"That's one too many."

"Concussion?"

"Yeah. Probably."

He sighed. "I remember the kids with the rifles, leaning against the truck. And we gave them cigarettes."

"What else?"

"A sign. We found the lane, and then . . . then those jerks showed up. We were moving forward." He shook his head, his gaze locked on hers.

"Daisy nipped your mare."

When Dylan smiled, she added, "But it wasn't Daisy's fault."

"It never is. That mare!"

"They were crowding us."

"The lane. . . it was like a funnel."

"I suspect that's exactly what it was."

"Where are we?"

"Franklin's." She peered more closely at his eyes.

"What are you looking at?"

"Your pupils. I think they're dilated."

"How can you tell?"

"Because I've been trained. Remember? Cade? Doc Turner? Logan?"

"Oh, yeah. Alpine." He seemed to suddenly notice the room, the chiminea, the couch pillows. "We're not in Alpine anymore."

"Nope."

"So the goons . . . are they Franklin's people?"

"I don't know, but if we thought we were going to get help here, then I think we're going to be sorely disappointed."

"It's okay."

Akule had started to move away, but Dylan reached for her hand, and she found she couldn't pull back. She was so very tired. Not just physically—that was hard enough to deal with. She was tired of people being assholes. She was weary from having to watch for danger from every direction. She was heartsick at what the world had become.

"We're going to find your brother."

Tears stung her eyes.

Dylan was lying on a stranger's couch. He'd been slugged by some guy with a pistol and thrown from his horse. His head had to be aching, and his body was going to be very sore.

But he wasn't thinking about those things.

He was thinking about her.

And wasn't that really the definition of friendship?

She stared down at her hand covered with his. "We're only halfway there."

"That's one way to look at it. On the other hand, we're halfway there."

An hour later they'd been moved to a small prefab home that sat a hundred yards away from the lodge. Franklin, his ex-wife, and their two young children lived in the small house adjacent to it. Franklin's ex-wife had raised a hand in greeting, and the kids had done the same, but they hadn't come over to say hello.

Keme found the entire situation beyond strange.

Dylan was asleep in the single bedroom, their horses were in the pasture, and all of their supplies were on the floor in front of them. At least they wouldn't be robbed blind. They might be killed then robbed, but. . . well, anyone intent on doing that would have to get past him. Anyone wanting their things or wanting to hurt him or his people . . . they would have to kill him first.

"You're sure it's okay if we stay here?" Keme wasn't convinced. He kept dragging his gaze around the room as if trying to anticipate what could go wrong next.

"For a day. Two at the most. Douglas isn't a fan of visitors, as you might have figured out."

"And he's your father-in-law?" Keme shook his head. "No wonder you and Cara divorced."

"He's a hard man to live with, but he's also kept Cara and the kids safe. I owe him for that. Even if I don't agree with his ways."

"What does that mean?" Akule asked.

Keme thought Franklin wouldn't answer.

He stared at the floor, then glanced toward the hall that led to the room where Dylan rested. Maybe he answered Akule's question because he thought that he owed them at least that much. After all, it was one of Douglas's cohorts that had bashed in Dylan's skull.

"You've heard of survivalist groups? Douglas Perkins has created a survivalist group on steroids and—in my opinion—any compassion he might have once had before June 6th has since been sacrificed for the cause."

"Give me an example." Keme wasn't merely curious.

He needed to understand the man they would have to deal with, and it was obvious that person was Douglas. He was in charge here. It wasn't a democracy, and Franklin didn't hold any of the power. He'd been able to gather that much in the last hour.

"An example. Okay. We had a pretty severe cold storm settle in this area three weeks ago. A family with a young girl—a sick young girl—came through the choke point."

"That's what you call it?" Akule exchanged a look with her father, shook her head, and closed her eyes for a moment.

He understood exactly what she was feeling.

They should have seen the trap.

Should have recognized the *choke point* for what it was.

Should have kept on riding past Franklin's place, past the lake, and north to Dallas even if it did mean riding into the unknown.

"Yeah. That's what we call it. So, this family came through the choke point. They'd been living in a tent at the lake, but the girl had a high fever, and the parents were scared. They were greeted about the same way you were." Some memory caught in Franklin's throat. He swallowed, pushed past it. "They were threatened. The dad was smacked around a bit, but he wouldn't back down. He insisted on seeing the guy in charge."

"Douglas."

"Douglas." Franklin stared down at his hands and then looked up—first at Akule, then at Keme.

It seemed to Keme that he was seeking forgiveness.

"Douglas turned them away. Said they should have prepared better. Insisted his men take them in the Gator back over to the lake."

"I guess that's better than making them walk back."

"Not really. He wasn't doing it to be compassionate. He wanted them off his property."

"And the girl?"

Franklin shook his head. "I walked over the next day, looking for them. I'd smuggled out some Tylenol and a little fruit juice, but. . . I was too late."

An uncomfortable silence filled the room.

Keme had come across plenty of bad people since June 6th. He'd fought against people that some might even call evil. And he'd come across an almost equal number of good people. But this was . . . different. This was preparation and experience wrapped in fear.

"I know Douglas sounds like a bad person, but his stance is understandable." Franklin was now speaking quickly, the words spilling out of him as if he needed to defend this situation he was caught up in and the people he'd aligned with. "That's what makes it so hard to confront. If he gives out medical supplies to every family that asks, he wouldn't have any left for his own family . . . for my family. Douglas predicted something exactly like June 6th would happen."

"How's that possible?"

"He's not a prophet. He didn't see the future. But he did understand that our dependence on technology had reached a tipping point. He understood, and he prepared for that eventuality in a way that few people did."

"Okay." Keme leaned forward, hands clasped, elbows on his knees. "Okay."

"Tell me about Alpine. How's Lucy?"

And that question was like a splash of cold water in Keme's face.

"Mom's dead," Akule said softly.

She looked at her dad, but he couldn't find his voice, couldn't find words or answers or the ability to describe the thing that had upended his life.

And Lucy's death had done that.

Not June 6th.

Not the lack of technology or government oversight or production of goods.

The absence of his wife, of his helpmate, of the person that he had depended on since he was nineteen years old—that had turned his life, his heart, inside out.

"She died in the battle of Marfa," Akule explained. "She died defending Alpine."

"I'm sorry. I didn't know."

"How could you?" Keme sat back on the couch, glanced down at their saddles and backpacks and supplies, then looked back up at Franklin. He pushed the memories of Lucy and the pain of that loss back down.

He locked it in a box in the middle of his soul.

"But things are good in Alpine now," Akule said. "It's not perfect. We need stuff. But the town has pulled together. We have a triage center. Our doctors are training students from the university. We have the Legacy Project—to document what is happening."

"And a school." Keme pulled in a steadying breath. "A

school, daycare, students who check on the elderly. Everyone who can work, does work. They pull their weight."

"We even have a restaurant."

He turned to look at his daughter. She sounded almost wistful. Almost homesick.

"My dad and Dylan, they ride the perimeter with other men and women."

Franklin looked as if he were trying to take in all they were saying, trying and failing. Of course, when he had left the Alpine area, the changes in their world were new and Alpine hung precariously in the balance. It still did, to some extent.

"You have a perimeter set up around Alpine? How is that any different than our choke point?"

"Because the perimeter also serves to help people who are seeking refuge." Keme's voice grew stronger. "A few months ago, we had a family racing toward Alpine. They were being chased by the Watchmen—a group of outlaws. The woman had been shot. There were three adults and two children in the car."

"She survived." Akule picked up the story. "They brought her to our triage center."

"If we'd turned them away. If we'd had a choke point. If we'd told them we couldn't help, Harper would have died. The entire group might have died."

"But they didn't. They became a part of Alpine. Cade practices medicine now—in Alpine. Liam helps with defense and security. And the kids. . ." Akule sighed. "They're good kids, and they'll have a chance because we let them in. We didn't try to choke them out."

"Things aren't perfect in Alpine." Keme stood now and walked to the window, but he turned back to Franklin when he spoke. "It's a better way, Franklin. I understand what you're saying, what Douglas is saying. There's a temptation to burrow down. To say, *what I've put back is for me and mine*."

"It's more than that though. My family is alive because of his attitude, because of his preparation. What kind of hypocrite would I be to judge him for that?"

Keme held up both of his hands, palms out. "I'm not saying to judge him. I'm saying there's a better way."

CHAPTER 9

Dylan insisted on joining the others for the meeting with Franklin's father-in-law that night. "He sounds like a jerk."

"Yeah. He is that and worse." Akule reached out and touched his arm. "Are you sure you're up to this? Because you can go back and sleep some more."

"Later. Let's get this over with."

Akule had wrapped strips of bandage around his head. He could feel the top of his hair flopping over it, and it irritated him that his Stetson no longer fit well. But he no longer wobbled when he walked. He'd stopped seeing two of everything. His head felt like someone had smashed it with a sledgehammer, but Akule had said he'd live.

She kept glancing at him, as if she was worried about him, and he liked that. He liked her being worried about him. Too bad it had taken a concussion for that to happen. Or maybe she'd cared all along, but hadn't wanted to let it show. Sometimes hiding your feeling was the safest thing to do.

He understood that.

They walked across to the lodge. Dylan tried to focus on

their mission, on Akule, on anything but the pounding in his skull. At least his head had stopped bleeding. He supposed that was something.

They met in the living room. There was a roaring fire that was doing a good job of warming the place. He could smell something cooking in the kitchen, but he knew they wouldn't be invited to dinner. Akule had given him a summary of the meeting with Franklin. This was a Hail Mary pass, as no one expected to receive much help from Douglas. But apparently the man was always on the look out for a good trade.

There was no council.

No group had been picked by the community to run things.

Douglas ruled the compound.

Franklin was already there. He sat in an overstuffed chair, looking uncomfortable. Looking like he didn't belong, and Dylan suspected he didn't. Franklin was caught between the proverbial rock and hard place. His family was here, but Franklin had finally admitted to Keme and Akule that he'd rather be in Alpine. He thought it was a better option.

Cara refused to go.

Franklin refused to leave his children.

Douglas and Phyllis Perkins sat in straight-backed chairs near the fire. Dylan, Akule, and Keme sat on the couch.

Douglas didn't waste any time. "Franklin has briefed me on your mission to find your son. While I'm sympathetic, there's nothing we can do to help you."

"You mean you won't help. Not you can't, but you won't." Keme's tone was calm, cool, nonjudgmental.

Dylan was impressed.

He was personally still pissed at getting bashed in the head. He wouldn't have been nearly as polite to this jerk who acted as if he were sitting on a throne.

"Correct. I won't."

"But you're open to a trade."

"If you have anything we need, which I doubt." Douglas bounced his fingertips together. "What you have to understand is that I'm responsible for all the people here at Camp Perkins—responsible for my wife, her mother, my daughter and her children."

Now he cast a patronizing look at Franklin. "Even my son-in-law, though legally he abandoned his role as protector to his family when he divorced her."

Franklin didn't respond.

Dylan suspected he'd heard this before.

Keme brought the conversation back to the matter at hand. "I believe there is a way you can help us. You must have a lot of resources at your disposal. You're part of a larger community."

"We have twelve ranches in total that chose to participate. Men and women who understood that America was at a crossroads. They sacrificed purchasing what most Americans consumed on a regular basis—new phones and cruise vacations and designer clothes. They saved their money instead, so they could put back supplies. Those supplies will see us through, if we're good stewards."

"All right. But you couldn't have thought of everything. There must be something that you need."

Douglas shrugged. "Possibly. What do you have?"

Yeah, he'd done this before.

Dylan had once gone to a pawn shop. He'd decided to sell his game console because his dad had left them and his mom was working two jobs and still there wasn't enough money each week. There was never enough. So he'd gone to the pawn shop, game console tucked into his backpack. As an adult, he understood the business model of a pawn shop. As a young teen, he'd been appalled to learn he'd only receive a fraction of what the game system was worth.

This reminded him of that.

Keme nodded at Akule. She dropped her pack to the floor and began pulling out what they had to trade. An hour earlier, they'd met and decided what they were willing to part with and what they needed to keep. It hadn't been easy. They didn't have that much, and they were still a long way from Dallas.

Akule laid the items on the coffee table.

The bottle of whiskey.

Another pack of cigarettes.

The jar of honey.

The diamond ring.

Chewing tobacco.

Douglas shook his head, but then he looked at his wife. She stood, walked to the coffee table, and knelt.

She fingered the diamond ring. Set it back down.

Picked up the jar of honey and the bottle of whiskey. Met Akule's gaze as she ran her thumbs over the label on the whiskey and the seal on the honey.

Turning to her husband, she said, "Both would help—for medicinal use." Then she set the items back on the table, stood, crossed the room ,and resumed her place next to Douglas.

"All right. She wants those two items. You can put the others up."

After Akule had done so, Douglas crossed his arms. "What do you want from us?"

"We want to get to Dallas."

"So Franklin said."

"And we know you can get us there."

This was the moment of no return. Franklin had shared about the trade route that his father-in-law had with the government or an arm of the government. It was something no one outside of Camp Perkins was supposed to know about. It was something Franklin could get kicked out for having shared.

Douglas sent his son-in-law a black look. "Say I could. I'd need more than a jar of honey and a bottle of whiskey."

"You saw what we had."

"I saw what you showed me."

"It's what we're willing to share."

"It isn't enough."

Dylan wanted to bolt. They didn't need this asshole's help. They could take the horses and leave. They *would* take the horses and leave.

But if there was a faster way to get to Dallas . . .

If there was a way to find Paco and his family and bring them home . . .

Dylan would have traded anything in Akule's pack for that.

He knew what it was like to have a broken, fragmented family. And he understood he couldn't make her family whole again. No one could. She would always feel the loss of her mother.

But, maybe—just maybe, they could accomplish this one thing. They could bring Paco home.

Douglas had gone back to bouncing his fingertips together.

Pompous ass.

"Let's say, for the sake of argument, that I could arrange transport. I would need something more from you."

"Like what?"

"Your mares and the mule plus the saddles."

Dylan froze. His mind froze. His thoughts froze.

His heart might have temporarily stopped.

"We can't give you our horses," Keme said. "We'd have no way home."

Douglas stood, walked to the fireplace, and tossed another log onto the blaze—as if to accentuate his abundance. There was no rationing of firewood here. They had plenty. He was holding all the cards, just like the guy who owned the pawnshop.

"You seem like an intelligent man, Mr. Lopez. Surely you have calculated the odds of finding your son, of even surviving such a trip. They're not good."

"We know the risk."

"I'll provide transport. You can be in Dallas this time tomorrow. In exchange, if you haven't returned in one month's time, I keep the horses, the mule, and the saddles."

Dylan thought Keme would say no. That he'd yell at the man or call him a fool or maybe simply laugh at him. That he wouldn't do this unimaginable thing.

Instead, Keme stood. "We'll need a few moments to talk—privately."

"Of course. You may use the back porch, where you were before."

THEY HAD BARELY STEPPED onto the sunporch when Akule turned on her dad. "We can't give him the horses. I won't do it."

Instead of arguing, Keme watched his daughter and waited.

She felt sick to her stomach.

She loved her brother and his family. She would do anything for them. She would give up Daisy for them. But it seemed to her if they did that, they were also giving up any chance of seeing Alpine again. "How would we get home? It's going to be difficult enough with Paco and Claire, Pete and Danny. How will we even stand a chance on foot?"

"Let's hold that question for a moment." Keme motioned toward the far side of the porch. When they had moved as far away from the living area as possible and were standing in a circle, he lowered his voice. "First of all, do you think he can do it? Could he get us to Dallas by this time tomorrow?"

"Maybe he has a plane," Dylan suggested. "We've seen a few fly overhead, even in Alpine. The planes didn't all stop flying on June 6h. FAA stopped. Fuel became hard to come by. But planes still work."

"Franklin didn't mention a plane, but he did mention a trade route." Akule rubbed a thumb over her bottom lip. "I think the persons they're trading with have trucks. That would line up with what Liam has told us about the fragmented groups of the military."

"Okay. So we agree that he can do what he says."

Dylan and Akule both nodded.

Her dad stared over her head, out the window, to something beyond. "He's saying if we can't get back in thirty days the animals are his. But what if we could make it back?"

"He's betting we won't." Dylan scowled at the wall, at the man on the other side of the wall. "I really don't like that guy."

"I never thought we could take the horses all the way into Dallas anyway," Keme said. "I was worried about where to leave them. Worried that even if we had a place, they'd be stolen. Here, they'll be safe. No one's getting past the choke point."

Akule rolled her eyes. Stupid paramilitary prick. Who was he to decide who would live and who would die? Who was he to play God?

And then Stella's words came back to her.

Life is hard, but God is good.

She still didn't know if she believed that. But here was an opportunity to get to Paco quickly. An opportunity she never would have guessed they'd be presented with.

"It won't be easy," she said. "But we still have other things to trade. Maybe we could find transportation back. Thirty days is a long time."

If they found Paco quickly.

If they could find anyone to trade with.

If, for once, things turned in their direction.

Keme lowered his voice even more, so that Akule had to step closer, as did Dylan. I felt like they were standing in a kind of huddle, heads bent, bodies close, hearts striving and reaching and set on the same goal.

"His weakness is his arrogance," Keme said. "And what does he have to lose? A month's worth of feed, of which I'm betting he has plenty."

"Do you think we can trust him to keep his word?" Dylan sounded doubtful.

"Yeah. People like Douglas Perkins, they're big on keeping their word. Even when it means turning away sick children."

Akule thought her father was right about that. Douglas Perkins considered himself to be a good man. A righteous man. A guy who was nearly always the smartest person in the room. "He'll want a backup plan. He won't just hand the horses and saddles over even if we do get back within the thirty days. He'll find some way to make it hard on us. Some obscure clause in the agreement."

"You're probably right. We'll allow him to think he's holding all the cards, but we'll prepare for what you're describing. We'll bring back something else that he needs. For now, we'll lie if we have to. We'll promise whatever he wants, and we'll get Paco and Claire and the kids here. From here, it's only two weeks to Alpine. We could be home by February."

Home by February.

Those words were too optimistic to even entertain, but what if her father was right? Akule could imagine the joy on Tanda's face, the tears in her grandparents' eyes. She could clearly see her brother and his family living in one of Alpine's vacated homes. Then she thought of Tanda and Logan and Stan Makowski who was in charge of patrols.

"We need to remember that Alpine needs all three horses, and Fiona belongs to the Scotts. We're gambling with our town's resources here."

"That's true." Her dad crossed his arms and stared out the window, then returned his gaze to her and Dylan. "We were entrusted with all three horses and the mule in order to bring back Paco and his family."

"The saddles themselves are a precious commodity," Dylan added.

"You're right. You're both right. We'll do everything in our power to return Fiona and to arrive back in Alpine with Texas Lady, Amber, and Daisy. But the Scotts and Stan knew the risks when they gave us the animals to use. They understood how bad it could get out here."

They must have looked like three people worrying over the most critical of decisions. And they were. But something had changed since they'd walked out into the sunroom. The possibility of what could happen had broken over the horizon. The possibility of seeing her brother in twenty-four hours had infused Akule with a crazy kind of energy. She knew it wouldn't be that easy. Knew it could take days or even weeks to locate him. But they'd be closer if they accepted Perkins' challenge. They'd be much closer.

"I'm in," Dylan said.

She suspected he wanted revenge for the wound on the back of his head. And Akule wanted revenge too. She wanted the good guys to win for once. And there was no doubt in her mind that they were the good guys. They were on the right side of things.

So she said the only thing she could say. "I'm in."

Her father slapped Dylan on the back and pulled her into a hug and then pulled Dylan into the same hug. And Akule felt safe. She felt connected. She felt like they could do this. Together, they could do this.

As one, they turned and walked back toward Douglas.

It was time to make a trade.

CHAPTER 10

Franklin was there to see them off. "I'm sorry about how this all played out."

"None of what happened was your fault," Keme said.

And it wasn't. Franklin hadn't instructed someone to clock Dylan. He certainly hadn't told his father-in-law to be a ruthless negotiator. Nope Franklin was simply caught up in something that he didn't know how to extricate himself from.

"You know you can always come back to Alpine. You'd be welcome there. We need good people like you."

The last sentence landed on Franklin like a punch. Keme and Franklin had never been terribly close. They'd been neighbors that waved at one another occasionally, once in a great while they'd sat outside together, complaining about slow internet and the price of groceries. But when Keme said that Franklin could come back to Alpine, would be welcome there, would be needed there. . . when he said those words Franklin had wrapped him in a bear hug, whispered, "Be careful," then walked off toward his small home.

The horse trailer left at eleven p.m. that night.

Douglas Perkins was not transporting horses.

Instead, the trailer was packed with square bales of hay. A small space in the middle had been left open for Keme, Akule, and Dylan. There was barely enough room for their bodies and their packs. Once they had climbed into the trailer, more bales of hay had been packed between them and the back door.

The truck was moving.

They'd be in Dallas in less than five hours.

Two men and a woman were riding in the cab of the truck. They all wore military fatigues—digital camo pattern, which was reputed to work well in any environment—desert, woodland. . . urban. Keme wondered if that was intentional. If someone higher up had decided that was the perfect camouflage for the challenges they faced. Or maybe it was simply what had been available in the barracks.

"Feels strange to be riding in a vehicle." Akule was perched on a half stack of hay bales. "Feels wicked."

She wiggled her eyebrows and Dylan laughed.

These two.

They bounced back from life's challenges. Akule and Dylan reminded Keme of giant beach balls that were occasionally pushed underwater. Nearly impossible to keep down. Full of life. Full of fight. Keme envied them their tenacity. He did not envy their inexperience, and make no mistake—both were naïve. In spite of what they'd already been through. In spite of the lifeless bodies in the abandoned vehicles, the need to make a wide arc around Sanderson, Dylan's concussion, the coldness of Douglas Perkins.

In spite of all of those things, they could smile.

That, in turn, made him smile.

"What are you grinning at?" Dylan laughed when Keme made a who-me gesture. "Yeah, you. You're grinning. I saw it."

"It's nice to be making good time for once."

The game clock had started. They had thirty days to find Paco and his family and make their way back to Camp Perkins. After thirty days, the animals became the property of Douglas Perkins, and they were all determined that would not happen.

"I'm surprised he went for it," Akule said. "Guess you were right, Dad. The guy's arrogant."

"Yeah, but what's up with the *bring him something* command? Bring him something. Like what? What exactly are we supposed to bring him? I know what I'd like to bring him." Dylan closed his hand in a fist.

Akule laughed.

Yeah, their adrenaline was pumping.

They needed to slow it down. Save the surge of energy for when they needed it, and Keme suspected they would need it.

"We'll find something," Keme said, sounding more certain than he felt. "I have no idea what, but we'll find something. He'll return our animals and our saddles. And we'll ride home to Alpine."

If only.

What was the expression his abuela used to say? *From your lips to God's ears.*

"Think our drivers are actually with the military?" Akule asked.

"Could be." Keme shrugged. "I guess it doesn't really matter. Maybe not what you and I think of Uncle Sam's military, but they're at least a part of some military. Or paramilitary."

"What does that word even mean?"

"Civilians organized in a military fashion." When Akule stared at Dylan in surprise he added, "Video games. You know. Old world."

"Yeah."

Which seemed to sober them up.

"We should try to get some sleep." Keme repositioned his backpack, which was digging into his sciatica causing a pain to creep down his leg. He turned his mind away from it. Closed his eyes. He could still hear Akule and Dylan talking in soft voices. Remembering times they'd been to Dallas. Wondering what it looked like now. Speculating on whether the city itself was still intact. Considering and dismissing ideas for how they were going to find Paco.

The rock of the trailer and the rhythm of tires against pavement and the events of the last two weeks pushed Keme from energetic anticipation into a deep sleep. He woke when the trailer jerked to a sudden stop. Scrubbing a hand over his face, he peered through the darkness at Akule and Dylan. They looked as confused as he felt.

Dylan was peering over one set of hay bales, out the small window, into the darkness.

Akule was doing the same on the opposite side of the trailer.

Keme moved to join them. Then, at the sound of voices, they all froze.

"Armstrong isn't letting anyone through."

"Since when?"

"Last night. He made a big show of force."

"We need to deliver this hay. We have paperwork."

"Give it to me. And I'll need to look in the back."

Akule and Dylan silently dropped to the floor, as did Keme.

They didn't dare to speak. Tried to quiet their breathing.

The back doors of the trailer made a squeal as they were opened. Keme held his breath, looked down at his hands, and was surprised to find he was gripping the Colt. He didn't remember pulling it from his holster.

"Looks good." He slammed the doors shut. "Stay here. I'll go and radio in for an alternate route."

It had been the driver of the truck speaking to the new person. Now he said in a low voice to one of the other two, "Better check on our passengers."

The doors were opened again, this time slowly, gently, quietly.

It was the younger man who spoke over the bales of hay. He was redheaded, freckled, and looked impossibly young to Keme.

"Everyone okay back there?"

"We're fine." Keme holstered his weapon.

"Might as well come out and stretch."

Keme motioned for the others to wait and wiggled his way through. "You're sure it's safe?"

"Yeah. Fowler's headed to get an approved alternate route for us. You have a good twenty minutes before he'll be back."

Keme turned to tell Akule and Dylan what the kid had said, but they were already up and moving toward him.

They tumbled out of the back of the trailer like pups out of a basket and as one, they turned to stare at the red, angry glow to the north and a little east. Even from this distance, he thought he could smell the smoke.

"What is that?"

"That?" The kid pulled off his cap, crushed the bill into a more pleasing shape, and stuck it back on his head. "That's Dallas."

"It's burning?" Akule pushed her way to the front of the little group.

"Yeah. It's been burning for a long time. Weeks, I guess."

"Why?" Dylan asked.

"How?" Keme realized they were closer to their destination than he'd thought. In fact, they were nearly to Cedar Hill. They could walk from here. Except there was the guy Armstrong, who was insisting they take another route.

"Depends on who you talk to as to who started it. There are different groups vying for control. Gangs, I guess. There's not really any fire department anymore. No water to fight fires with. Once something goes up in flames it tends to spread."

"So downtown is..." Akule turned to stare at him. "What is it?"

"Uninhabitable, if that's what you're asking."

Keme pivoted to the northwest. "And Fort Worth?"

"Apparently it's doing better than Dallas. Bunch of cowboys there who didn't mind enacting marshal law quickly and completely."

"But Dallas is burning." Dylan looked as if he couldn't quite wrap his mind around the idea.

"As far as we've heard, nearly every large city is. Course that's mostly rumor and conjecture. I don't know anyone who's actually been out of Texas since June 6th."

Keme didn't know what to say to that. He felt as if he were going to be sick. He'd never been able to handle destruction. He hadn't even watched violent movies. It had all seemed so pointless to him. And yeah, he thought he'd toughened up over the last six months.

Maybe not.

"If you ask me, which you didn't, you folks would have been better off staying back where you came from."

"We're looking for my brother." Akule's voice was soft but resolute. Akule wouldn't let a burning city stand between her and Paco.

And Keme was proud of that. He was proud that his children cared for one another. He realized that wasn't always the case in every family. "Have you heard anything about Cedar Hill? That's where my son used to live."

"Heard there's an encampment out by the lake there." He shook his head. "My boss would like to clear those pockets out, but there's only so much one regiment can do, and we're working from north of the Dallas metroplex. Not from the south."

"Why do you need the hay?" Dylan asked.

"Well, the vehicles work, but fuel is scarce. Horses have been a good supplement to our transportation problems. Not that I know how to ride one." He laughed, then appraised Dylan. "You look like you do."

"Yeah. I can ride a horse."

The guy who had been driving whistled once, and the young man in front of them held up a finger. "Wait here."

They couldn't make out what was said.

So, they waited. It was that or run, and Keme didn't relish the idea of running off into the darkness with Fowler running patrols and blocking roads.

It seemed to take forever, but it didn't. Probably two to three minutes, and then they heard the distinctive sound of footsteps walking toward them again. Then redheaded kid was back. "We have a new route. If you still want to go to Cedar Hill, we can get you pretty close."

"Thank you." They piled back into the trailer, but this time no one slept. The driver picked up speed, now certain of his route.

Twenty minutes later they were dropped off on the west side of town.

The kid held the doors open as they made their way out of the trailer, brushing off hay and stretching out the kinks in their backs.

"We're headed north from here," the kid said.

"Thank you." Keme shook his hand. "Didn't get your name."

"Archie. Archie Gifford, and yeah—my mom was a fan of the cartoon."

"Thank you, Archie." Dylan also shook his hand.

Akule did the same. "I hope you get the hay to your horses."

"I hope you find your brother."

"So do we, Archie. So do we."

The trailer pulled away. The three from Alpine stood there for a moment, transfixed by the red glow on the horizon. Dallas burning. They were closer to it now. The acrid smell of uncontrolled flames filled the air. A veil of destruction draped the metroplex.

Keme had initially doubted the wisdom of their journey. He now accepted that Akule's instincts had been correct. They needed to find Paco, Claire and the boys. They needed to take them home to Alpine.

KEME HAD BEEN to visit Paco at his Cedar Hill home twice. He'd planned to go more often. He'd told himself there would be a lot of chances. Keme had told the others that Douglas Perkins was arrogant, but hadn't they all been?

He had.

He'd thought he had all the time in the world.

It wasn't yet dawn, but the sky was lightening.

"We could find a place to hunker down." Keme turned in a slow circle.

They were standing at the intersection of Highway 67 and Lake Ridge Parkway. Continuing along the highway did not look like a viable route. Abandoned cars stretched as far as he could see. As for the nearby neighborhood, a few houses were close enough to see the rooftops and windows. Glass was broken out of some. Windows had been left open and drapes fluttered in the cold winter wind. In places, front doors had been left open and snow had piled up in the entryway

It seemed that nothing here was inhabited. The people who had lived here had fled. "We could go into one of those houses and rest, or we could push on. How do you two feel?"

"I'm good," Dylan said, wincing as he pushed his cowboy hat onto his head.

"Akule?"

"Good. What about you? Did you get enough sleep?"

"I got a few winks."

Which caused Akule and Dylan to laugh.

"You were so out before that first stop. If we'd had anything to make spit wads out of..." Dylan raised his hand, and Akule softly high-fived him, pressing the palm of her hand against his.

"But we didn't. So you didn't swallow any paper."

"I'm not sure I believe you."

"Not the question." Akule's tone turned serious and she gave him a severe no-nonsense look. "The question is do you feel rested?"

"Enough," he said. "Let's do what we came here to do."

The sun had properly risen, but the day was cold with a stiff north wind.

"We'll go to Paco's house first," he said. "Maybe he left a note or something."

"In the movies they usually paint a note on the wall." When Akule and Keme turned to stare at Dylan, he added, "You know, zombie apocalypse and all that. People always paint notes on the wall. That way you'll see it, and it won't, like, blow away or something."

It occurred to Keme that the Akule who had left Alpine would have mocked Dylan. Maybe slapped him on the back of the head. Of course, now he had a bandage around his head, so she'd never do that.

But Keme could tell that she was more amused than irritated. She bumped her shoulder against his—hard, sending him stumbling and laughing.

There didn't seem to be any reason to move quietly.

But suddenly, instinctively, they were.

As they crossed Highway 67, skirted around the high school and entered the neighborhood where Paco lived, all three grew silent. Moved stealthily. Scanned their surroundings.

They were a few houses from Paco's when trouble found them.

Keme was leading. Dylan in the middle. Akule at the back.

Single file.

Down the street.

Keeping close to the houses and the shadows.

Keme heard a grunt from behind as if the air had been knocked out of someone. He turned to find an ill-kempt twenty-something with his arm around Akule's neck and a blade pointed toward her chest.

Keme and Dylan pulled their guns as one.

As if they'd been doing this all their lives.

"Wouldn't," the guy spat, then grinned revealing teeth decayed by neglect or drugs or both. "Not if you want her to live."

Keme's mind considered and discarded options.

They could shoot the guy, but that would alert others.

They could overpower him, but not with his arm wrapped around Akule's neck.

Fortunately, Akule didn't wait to be saved.

She drove her elbow into her assailant's ribs with a force that left him clutching his side. Then she turned and kicked him hard as he collapsed to the ground. Then she pulled her weapon.

"Idiot."

He immediately curled in a ball, groaning and shouting, "Don't hurt me. Don't hurt me."

"Shut up before you alert the entire neighborhood."

The man peered up at him quizzically, then resumed clutching his stomach and moaning.

Dylan had picked up the guy's knife and secured it in his pack.

"Let's get him inside," Keme said.

They moved into the nearest house.

"Make sure no one's here."

Dylan and Akule moved off in opposite directions. The home was massive and two stories. They cleared the upstairs. Checked the garage. The downstairs rooms. When they walked back into the living room, nodding that all was good, Keme focused on the punk in front of him.

Keme pushed the guy—not gently but definitely not with all of his force. He folded like a popped balloon.

"He isn't so tough without his knife," Akule's hand rubbed her chest, as if she could still feel the point of the weapon.

Dylan sank into an overstuffed chair. "Can you believe this guy?"

"What's your name?" Akule asked.

"Why would I tell you?"

Akule squatted beside him and waited until he met her gaze. "You had a knife pointed at my heart, and I didn't kill you. Now what is your name?"

"Stan," he muttered, aiming for defiant but coming up short. "Stanley Evans."

"Stan the man." Dylan kept his weapon trained on the guy.

Akule perched on the arm of the couch.

Keme took lead in the interrogation. "What are you doing in this neighborhood?"

"Looking for stuff."

"Like?"

"I don't know. Anything. Food. Whatever."

"Where is everyone?"

"Gone. Anyone with any sense left."

Keme resisted the urge to point out that Stan was still there. "Where did they go?"

"Some to the camp at the lake. Others...just gone. I don't know, man. My stomach hurts." He leaned over and clutched the area that Akule had kicked.

"I didn't even kick you that hard."

"Yeah, but you have those boots on, and besides that I'm hungry."

"Give him something."

Akule drew back in surprise.

"Give him something, Akule. And in exchange, Stanley Evans is going to give us information."

He devoured the jerky and the water, then eyed Akule's backpack as if wondering what else was in there. She shook her head, once, and his shoulders fell.

"Tell us about the camp at the lake."

"It's like, I don't know, a work camp. I guess."

"A work camp?"

"Yeah. You can go in, but you can't come out."

"And most of the people in this neighborhood went there?"

"Not all. Lots were killed. You know, when the thing that happened, happened."

"And the rest? The ones who weren't killed?"

"Fled. Either out of town or to the camp. They didn't know then how it was there. No one knew."

"Okay. So how is it you're still out wandering the streets of Cedar Hill?"

"I work for Morales."

"Who's Morales?"

"Head of the underneath. Under something. Underground."

It was the first thing he'd said that offered a possibility. It was the first thing he'd said that they could use.

"You're going to take us to him."

"Her," Stan corrected. He shifted uncomfortably, then whined, "Not supposed to be out in the day. Camp people do their rounds. Try to catch folks."

"Guess we'll have to be careful then."

Akule cleared her throat. "Paco's first?"

"Yeah. Paco's first. C'mon, Stanley. We have a stop to make."

Stanley grumbled but the food and water seemed to have revived him a bit.

Keme was reminded of the drug users in Alpine who had gone through withdrawal in the days and weeks following June 6th. Tanda and Miles and Logan had set up a rehab of sorts in one of the local motels. A place for them to go through the sweats and chills and insomnia and exhaustion.

Some hadn't made it. They'd fled out into the desert, convinced they could find what they needed there. Others had simply curled into a ball, as Stan had, and after days and weeks of refusing to eat they had died.

But a good portion of those people had come through the agony of withdrawal and rejoined society. They weren't perfect people. They carried the same baggage that had lead them into the drug culture.

But maybe they were changed because they'd peered over the edge of their existence and seen that there was no longer any way to numb the pain they longed to escape. Maybe because there hadn't been another option, they'd survived and grown stronger and learned to work. It had been one of the few bright spots that resulted from June 6th. Those on the edge of society were forced back into the arms of society. There was no other way to survive.

He didn't know which Stanley would have been in Alpine. A survivor? Or one who succumbed to his addictions? But he'd lived through whatever had happened in Cedar Hill. If someone like Stanley Evans could survive, Keme was absolutely sure that his son was alive and well.

All they had to do was find him.

CHAPTER 11

Dylan kept an eye on Stan-the-man as Akule and Keme walked through Paco's home. Touching photographs. Straightening things that had been thrown about. Brushing broken glass to the side.

Those things were futile.

Instinctive maybe.

They all knew there would be no coming back to this house. It was huge and would be impossible to heat. In fact, he didn't even see a fireplace. It had been built for central heat and air. The ceilings were tall, the floors covered with some sort of fancy tile. Each room was twice as large as it needed to be, or so it seemed to Dylan. He couldn't imagine four people living in this place.

It also looked as if it had been ransacked more than once.

Akule and Keme walked slowly through each room, straightening and tidying. Futile gestures, but Dylan understood it was something they needed to do. As Dylan watched, Akule picked up a family photo that had been knocked to the floor. She studied it a moment, then carefully removed the photo from the broken frame. She held it up for Dylan to see.

The photo showed a guy who looked a little like Keme but more like Lucy. His hair was lighter. His face shaped like his mother's. The woman in the photo was also fair-headed. She was all made up like the photo had been professionally done, and he guessed it had been. Both of the kids were laughing—a boy who was old enough to be in school and a younger boy.

It was a moment in time.

A staged moment probably. Almost certainly.

But it was also genuine. Anyone could see that by looking at the smiles. This had been a happy family. A family who had no idea that the world was about to change.

Dylan didn't doubt for a moment that those very thoughts were going through Akule's mind. How was it that he knew her so well? That they had become so close in such a short time? Perhaps the shared experiences of danger and desperation did that to people.

Keme called out from the kitchen. "Found his note."

Akule slipped the photograph into her pack.

Dylan prodded Stanley with his foot. The man rose with a sigh and stumbled into the next room. It was a small kitchen considering the size of the house, and the room felt crowded with all three of them gathered around the kitchen counter.

"It's not paint on a wall, but it's close." Keme nodded to Dylan. "Guess you learned something from those disaster movies."

Dylan wasn't so sure about that.

In the movies, the desperate characters always found pop tarts or cans of cola or a fully stocked Cabela's. They'd found an idiot named Stanley and a note from Paco. Not paint on the wall. Permanent marker on the kitchen counter.

Gone to the encampment at Joe Pool.

That was it.

No explanation.

No clue as to when they'd left.

Or if they'd all survived.

"Guess he was in a hurry." Akule ran her fingertips over the words. "Or maybe he was afraid to say more."

"At least we know that's where he is." Keme turned to Stanley. "Now you're going to take us to Morales."

"We should wait. Until tonight."

"We're not waiting." Keme walked toward Stanley, backing him up until he was pressed against the refrigerator that no longer worked. "We're going now, and you're going to take us there. And if you walk us into a trap, we're going to kill you before anyone manages to kill us."

Stanley swallowed so hard that his Adam's apple bobbed. "Sure. Whatever, man."

He led them back to the state highway. They crossed at a different spot from where Archie's group had dropped them off. They crept along the edge of the street. Suddenly, Stanley froze like a rabbit that had been spied by a hawk.

Everyone stopped.

Everyone waited.

And then there was the distinct whine of a Gator moving down one of the side roads. Stanley waited for a full minute before moving again.

Stanley had some skills.

He might not have a strong moral compass, but he'd figured out how to survive in this ravaged town.

Once they were three blocks beyond the highway, he picked up his pace, taking them down a road that must have been in need of repaving in the best of times. Fifteen minutes later he angled away from the road onto what looked to Dylan like a deer trail. Were there deer in this area? He didn't think so. Then again, maybe the wildlife was already reclaiming what had once been theirs.

After walking through the woods another mile, he stopped and whistled twice. The answering whistle was immediate.

They stepped out between a chapel and a lodge, walked until they intersected a main road, and were met by two guys holding machine guns. Both looked like military types—jacked abs, buzzed haircuts, heavy artillery including bulletproof vests.

"What you got for us, Stanley?"

"Not what. Who. My name is Keme Lopez, and we're here to see Morales."

"No problem, but you'll have to give us your weapons."

Which to Dylan seemed like a very chancy thing to do.

This time there wasn't a vote though.

Keme handed over his Colt and his back-up, which was a Browning.

Akule gave them her Sig Sauer.

"Backup piece?"

"I don't need a backup piece."

The guy shrugged and turned to Dylan.

He didn't like it but now didn't seem like the time to argue. Their thirty-day clock was ticking. Keme and Akule were depending on him. Besides, he could fight without a firearm. He handed over his Smith and Wesson as well as Stanley's knife.

The guy must have recognized the knife because he sent a questioning look to Stanley, who simply shrugged.

One of Morales's men led them down the road. The other walked at the back with Stanley.

The buildings they passed looked deserted.

Why weren't people living here?

Why weren't the families trapped at the lake here instead?

And who was this Morales person?

Akule glanced his way, and Dylan admitted none of those questions because none of those answers mattered. What mattered was that they were one step closer to finding Paco.

AKULE WASN'T sure what she expected to see when they stepped in Morales's office. Maybe a Marine sergeant. But not a short, slight woman who looked as young as she was. Not that.

As for Morales, she didn't seem a bit surprised when they all trooped into her office.

"Duke. Milo." She stood and walked around the desk. "And Stanley." Her eyes moved to Akule, her dad, her friend.

She didn't ask what they were doing there.

Didn't ask if they were armed.

It was obvious to Akule that they had a system in place, and it worked. Morales, whoever she was, trusted Duke and Milo. And she wasn't threatened by Stanley's presence. Who would be?

"Take Stan to the mess hall."

"You got it, Boss."

It was funny seeing the bulked-up guys calling this small woman boss. But there was something about her that conveyed firmly *I'm in charge here.*

"My name is Isabella Morales."

"Keme Lopez." Her father stepped forward and shook the woman's hand. "This is my daughter, Akule, and our friend, Dylan."

Morales shook hands with each of them in turn. Then, cocking her head, she asked, "Are you seeking sanctuary?"

"No. Not that." Keme glanced around the office.

There wasn't a lot to it other than a local map and a state map pinned to a wall.

"We're here to find my son, and we were hoping you could help us."

They all sat, near an old-fashioned iron stove that heated the space remarkably well. The chairs had obviously been pulled from other rooms. They were a mish-mash of furniture. The warmth of the stove felt like bliss. Being out of the north wind, even for just a moment, raised Akule's mood.

Helped her believe that anything was possible.

Helped her reclaim the hope that what they'd come so far to accomplish was a thing that could be done.

As Keme explained their mission, Akule studied Morales.

Maybe older than she'd at first thought, but definitely under thirty. More muscular than she appeared. At one point she picked up a log to toss into the iron stove, her sleeve pulled away from her wrist, and Akule noticed the muscles in her forearm. She was as jacked-up as the men Duke and Milo. She simply hid hers under long-sleeved camo.

Her hair was somewhere between dark brown and black and was braided down her back. Her soft brown eyes focused completely on them. And running from her right temple to her chin was a very jagged, fairly new scar.

"Okay," she said. "I suppose it narrows things down to know your son is in Camp Penn, but it still won't be easy to find him."

"We didn't expect easy."

"Apparently not, if you came all the way from Alpine."

"Why do you call it Camp Penn?" Dylan asked.

"There's an old farm at the state park, located on this side of Joe Pool Lake. We think Will Martin picked the spot because of that farm and the fact that the lake provides him an easily protected border on one side. There's also a marina there with quite a few boats. Probably some of Martin's people are housed in those boats. As for the workers, they mostly live in tents.

"My brother...my nephews are living in a tent?" Akule worked to keep the despair out of her voice.

"Unless he's been promoted to staff." Morales put the last word in quotation marks. "He'd have to go along with some pretty cold-blooded dealings for that to happen."

"My brother would never do that."

"Then he's in the tents."

"Why are they there?" Dylan asked. "This looks like a big place. Why aren't they here? In fact, what is this place?"

Morales smiled, but Akule noticed the sadness behind that expression. What had happened to this woman? Why was she here? And how could she possibly help them find Paco?

"This facility is the Mt. Lebanon Baptist Encampment. It housed as many as twelve hundred people—youth camps, marriage retreats, that sort of thing. The most we've ever had here is a couple dozen, and then only for a night or two."

"No disrespect intended..." Keme again glanced around the room, then focused his gaze on the woman sitting in front of them.

The woman who, Akule knew, might hold the key to finding Paco.

"How did you come to be in charge here?"

"I was home on leave before deploying to my next assignment. U.S. Army. E-4 Specialist. After the grid went down, I attempted—without success—to rejoin my unit."

"Without success because..."

"As far as I could ascertain, it no longer exists." She waved that part of her story away. "When we became convinced the grid wasn't coming back, which was pretty quickly, we decided to head west. My cousins have a place in the panhandle." Isabella Morales didn't look away. Her voice never wavered. "The first night out, my parents were killed, and I was left for dead."

She didn't point to the scar.

She didn't have to.

Everyone in that room understood that someone had knifed her, then left her to bleed out.

"Milo and Duke were pararescue, United States Air Force. They found me, brought me here."

"Wow." Dylan ran a hand across the back of his neck. "Just. . . wow."

"They didn't want to leave me, and for the first few weeks, I was in no condition to travel. While we were holed up here, people would occasionally stumble into camp. We'd resupply them as best we could and send them on their way."

"No one wanted to stay?"

"The entire metroplex had become a scene of total destruction. No one wanted to stay. Everyone was fleeing. We helped when we could. We established an underground."

"Why is that even necessary?" Keme sat back, crossed his arms and frowned at a spot on the far wall. "Why do people need an underground to leave the metroplex?"

"People are resources, and they're in short supply."

To Akule that made sense.

Able-bodied folks might be hard to come by. They might not want to work. They might have to be forced into it. She thought of those early days in Alpine—when the art culture and the ranching culture had clashed. She thought of what Harper and Cade had seen north of the Guadalupe Mountains —a tent city full of people who weren't allowed to leave.

"Tell us how Camp Penn works."

"At first, people sought refuge there. Then, when they understood what the conditions were, they tried to leave and couldn't. Martin had sealed the place up tight and placed armed guards at every exit."

"How is that worth it? He has to feed them, house them..." Akule's words stumbled to a halt as she thought of Paco and Claire and the boys living in a tent in the middle of winter. If Martin had been quick to react, he could have broken into any camping store and had as much camping gear as he could load into a truck. And Paco might have thought there was safety in numbers.

"We only know what people coming out have told us, and that's slowed to virtually nothing the last month. But, from what they said, Martin is growing crops at the farm using mostly women and children for the labor. He has boats and nets for fishing, which is mostly done by teens. The adult men and stronger women take on the jobs that Martin has contracted to do. We don't know who is doing the contracting, what the job is, or how they're being paid. But something is making it worth Martin's time."

Dylan looked like Akule felt. As if he were trying mightily to catch up. "The people you said were seeking sanctuary...where are they from if they're not from the camp?"

"Those houses you passed may have looked empty, but there are still people in some of them, hiding, using the last of their supplies. The more desperate they become, the more likely they are to try and flee. Which is why we use people like Stan to locate them and bring them here."

"Stan put a knife to my throat. Not what you'd expect from a scout looking for refugees."

Morales's posture stiffened and her right hand balled into a fist. It was the first sign of anger that she had shown. "He and I will have a talk—again. If Stan doesn't get on board with our program, with our ways, he will be forced out of the area. Even if that means I have to ride west on a horse and leave him on the side of the road."

Keme sighed deeply, rubbed at his neck, then finally raised his gaze to Akule's. She nodded once, as did Dylan.

"It sounds like you're doing important work here," he said. "But we came to find my son, and that's what we plan to do. I'm sorry that we wasted your time."

Morales smiled and when she did, it seemed to Akule that the scar nearly melted away. "Oh, I didn't say I couldn't help. I said what you're attempting won't be easy." She stood, walked over to the wall map, and tapped the spot labeled Cedar Hill State Park.

"Milo and Duke can sneak you into the area tonight. Three or four in the morning works best. You can expect people walking patrols, but they aren't exactly alert or particularly motivated. The shine has gone out of Camp Penn."

"And then what do we do?" Akule had joined her at the map. Her brother was there, right at that point on the map where Morales was tapping the green spot next to the blue.

"Then you find a way in, get him out, and bring him here. We'll put you in our underground system and help you find a way back home."

"Sounds easy when you say it that way." Dylan had joined them at the wall.

As had Keme. "We're so close. We can do this. I know we can."

Which summed up what Akule was feeling.

They hadn't come this far to be defeated by a would-be king called Martin.

CHAPTER 12

They were directed to a bunkhouse close to the office. Their firearms lay on their beds, along with three clean towels and a single small bar of soap like what you would find in a hotel. Or would have, before June 6th.

The water was in a bucket in the bathroom.

Both the water and the bathroom felt to Keme like the temperature of a walk-in freezer. In fact, a thin layer of ice had formed on top of the water. The last thing he wanted to do was strip off his clothes. On the other hand, he hadn't really cleaned up since leaving Alpine.

Akule went next, grimacing when she stepped past him and into the cold bathroom.

Dylan went last, claiming that he'd once bathed in a cold creek and this couldn't be any worse than that. They heard his yelp when the cold water first hit his skin. Akule and Keme laughed. It was strange, how you could laugh at something when your heart was hanging in the balance.

They didn't speak of what they were about to attempt to do. They didn't bother to calculate the odds that they'd be bringing Paco and Claire, Pete and Danny with them in a few hours. They certainly didn't discuss what they'd do if this all went terribly wrong.

It was two in the afternoon, and Keme didn't think he'd be able to sleep.

He didn't think Akule and Dylan would even catnap.

But they weren't superheroes. They were young adults. Their adrenaline had spiked hours ago, and they were fast asleep even before Keme. When he closed his eyes, it was like taking a step off a cliff into the dark. He was gone.

They woke to a soft knock on the door. Morales stepped inside with a tray. "Hot coffee in the thermos. Granola bars were the best I could do for food. Train leaves in twenty minutes."

The train was actually five horses that had clearly seen better days, stamping and snorting under a January night sky adorned with millions of stars. Keme thought of the fine mares they'd left back in San Angelo...Daisy and Amber and Texas Lady. Fiona the mule. He vowed in his heart, again, that he would reclaim the animals. He didn't have a plan for transporting five adults and two children on three mares, couldn't even envision how they'd make it from Cedar Hill to Douglas's compound in San Angelo.

He'd think of something.

They walked the horses through the brush that bordered the east side of the encampment, mounted up, and rode north then northeast. Milo, the slimmer of the two men, led.

Akule, Dylan, and Keme followed.

Duke brought up the rear.

They moved quietly along a path that had clearly been staked out sometime before. Behind neighborhoods. Across small creeks. Down deserted streets. Eventually they made their way through a small, private college campus.

No people.

No animals that Keme could see.

Everyone and everything had fled.

On the far side of the campus, Milo pulled his horse to a stop. The others crowded in as close as they could get. When he spoke, it was in a soft voice, as if someone might be listening. Or perhaps that had simply become his habit.

"Morales has authorized me to leave the horses with you, but in my opinion you'd be better off proceeding on foot."

Keme once again sought consensus from Akule and Dylan.

All agreed and the three from Alpine dismounted, handing over the horses' leads.

"Parallel the road and continue north. Martin has guards walking the perimeter, but they're lackadaisical at best."

Dylan voiced the question they were all struggling with. "If the guards are so inept, why don't more people leave?"

"Martin has convinced them there's nowhere to go," Duke said. "He's convinced them that it could be worse."

Milo's horse stepped left. He reached forward and patted the gelding with a hand, but his attention was on Keme's group. "You have a little more than a mile to cover from here to the gate of the state park. We've come seven miles from the Mount Lebanon facility. Can you find your way back to us?"

"Yes." Keme was certain they could. He'd paid close attention to the route they'd taken. They could get back to the encampment.

If they didn't get shot first.

Or knifed.

Or captured.

"We will."

"I expect you to do exactly that."

"It might take a day," Akule said. "Or more."

"We'll still be there."

"Whistle twice when you come in the back way." Duke grinned. "Wouldn't want to shoot you by accident."

And then Milo and Duke were gone.

Keme realized anew what a strange journey they were on. A journey that brought them across the paths of terrible people willing to do unimaginable things. A journey that also brought them to new friends.

Within forty minutes they were crouched in the bushes, peering through their night vision binoculars. He saw the guard, saw the person stop to light a cigarette, then lean against the south side of a building to smoke it. He was protected from the north wind there. There was a good chance the man would fall asleep.

So, unmotivated guards exactly as they'd been told.

A point in their favor.

He heard Akule's sharp intake of breath and saw her pass the binoculars to Dylan, who pulled them away as if in disbelief, then peered through them again.

They weren't close to the guard but had decided to remain silent while they reconnoitered. Tracing their steps back another quarter mile, they formed a tight circle in a stand of Oak trees.

"What?" Keme asked. "What did you see?"

"Tents," Dylan said.

"Hundreds." Akule's voice was grim. "Hundreds of tents."

All three agreed it would be prudent to spend more time watching the camp and assessing their options. An hour later, they heard what sounded like a bugle call. Saw the families in the tents begin to stir. Within thirty minutes of waking, the men had walked off in one direction, women and children in another, teens in a third.

The group from Alpine continued watching.

Their break came at ten that morning. They were again

crouched down in the bushes, glassing the area with their binoculars, praying to see something that would give them an opening.

An old man shuffled into view. Apparently he'd been assigned clean-up duty. He pulled a wagon filled with a large trash can and cleaning supplies. They followed him down the length of the fence that bordered the state park, stopping when he stopped at one of the camp bathrooms. All of the tent occupants had risen hours ago and gone off to their various jobs. The guards had left with the workers. The old man seemed to be alone.

His back was stooped.

His white beard hung to his chest.

He moved with the despondency of someone who knew that what they were doing didn't matter, that they had no choices left in life, and that there was probably only a little time to endure the hardships he faced.

He moved like someone who had received a death sentence.

Akule insisted on being the one to climb through the fence and confront him as he came out from cleaning the bathroom.

They couldn't hear what she said, but as they watched, she spoke to the man and then waved toward the fence.

The old man shook his head and remained rooted to the spot.

She put a hand on each of his arms, waited for him to look at her, and spoke again.

This time the old man's shoulders dropped even more, but he nodded, and he moved in the direction that she'd indicated.

When the old man stood in front of them, Keme realized this situation was even worse than he'd imagined. The guy's clothes were tattered. His skin was chapped by the cold. His beard was matted, and he didn't look as if he'd had a good meal since June 6th. He also smelled.

Keme didn't waste any time. "We're here to find my son. He's with a woman and two small boys. He's living in this camp. His name is Paco."

"I don't know anyone's name." His voice was soft, submissive, resigned, and his gaze remained fixed on the ground.

"We need you to help us find him."

"I can't."

"You can. We've come a very long way, and we're not leaving without him."

The old man shook his head. "Lots of people in the camp. Once everyone comes back, we're not allowed to talk. And the guards return with them. What you're saying—it can't be done."

"It can be. All you have to do is slip him a note."

"But I don't even know who he is."

"He's this guy." Akule pulled a photograph from her pack, the same picture she'd taken from Paco's house.

There was something odd in the way the old man took one look at the picture, glanced up at Keme and Akule and Dylan, then back down to the picture.

"You know him," Akule said.

He didn't bother denying it.

"What is your name?"

"Joshua."

Akule pulled a small note pad and pen from her pack and passed it to her father.

Keme stared at it a moment, then began to write.

He showed the note to Akule and Dylan. Both nodded.

We're here to take you home.

1 a.m.

Follow Joshua.

Keme folded it once, then again. "Give that to my son, please. Then bring him and his family back here at one a.m."

Joshua took the note, but he didn't immediately put it in his pocket. When he looked up, his gaze was sharp, clear. So, the old-man demeanor had been a mask he wore, perhaps a way to stay safe.

"If I do this for you, I want something in return."

Akule again began pawing through the contents of her backpack. "We have cigarettes, tobacco, a little food..."

Joshua held up his hand to stop her. "I want to go with you."

They looked at one another in surprise.

Dylan finally spoke up. "That's a bad idea, Joshua."

Keme thought that perhaps Dylan was still seeing the old man that they'd been watching for over an hour. But that man had gone, evaporated into the air like a figment of their imagination. Someone different stood before them now.

"There are no guarantees if you go with us," Dylan was saying. "We'll be walking for a good bit of the trip. It's not going to be easy."

"I'll deliver your note. But only if I can go with you."

Keme caved quickly.

If the old guy wanted out, that was his business. Who were they to tell him where he could or couldn't go?

"All right," Keme said. "But we won't be responsible for you. We're here to rescue my son and his family. That's our priority. We know someone who can probably help you. We're returning there first. Once we're at her camp, our obligation to you is fulfilled."

"Deal."

Joshua climbed back through the fence with the agility of a much younger man.

"Real Benjamin Button, that one." Dylan reached for his water bottle and took a long drink.

Akule's voice was full of amusement, though her eyes were still on Joshua's retreating form. "You watched *Benjamin Button*?"

"Hello? Senior English."

"That's right. We had to read it, watch the Brad Pitt version, and then write a paper."

"Pure torture writing that paper, but the story kinda stays with you. Old guy. Gets younger and younger until... whatever happened to him?"

"He becomes a kid again, while the woman he loved..."

"Kate Blanchett."

"She becomes an old woman. It wasn't a story with a happy ending." Akule shot a glance at Dylan. "But I know what you mean. Joshua seemed almost spry when he returned to camp."

"Yeah." Keme nodded toward a cove of trees where they could rest and remain well hidden. "You two get some rest. I'll take the first shift."

Because he couldn't possibly sleep.

It wasn't only that they'd had a solid seven hours of rest in the bunkhouse. He was still exhausted. He honestly thought when he made it back home, back to Alpine, he'd be able to sleep for a week straight. But not now. Not while his son and daughter-in-law and two grandchildren were on the other side of that fence.

Dylan couldn't begin to fathom what Akule was going through, and he said as much to her.

"I think you can," she answered. "Haven't you ever imagined your dad coming home?"

"Even in my wildest dreams that wouldn't be a great reunion."

"Why is that?"

"He deserted us." Dylan lay back in the leaves, his head resting on his pack, his revolver close at hand just in case. "Sure, I've imagined asking him *why* and *how could he* and *didn't he care at all.* But I've never seen myself throwing my arms around his neck in relief at the sight of him."

And that was what he saw Akule doing.

There had been a thrumming energy coming from her since they'd spotted the tents hours earlier.

"I guess I get that," she said. "But maybe he thought you and your mom would be better off without him."

"Why would he think that?"

"I don't know." She lay down too, close enough that he could have reached for her hand, but he didn't. He'd accepted a very long time ago that he had a crush on Akule Lopez, and maybe—just maybe—she was beginning to have feelings for him.

It was still a maybe though.

No need to ruin things by jumping the gun.

"I think Paco initially left Alpine because he thought it would be better for our family."

"Explain that to me."

"He didn't embrace my father's ideas. Didn't really want to know anything about our Kiowa heritage. He thought all that stuff was unimportant. That my dad and my grandparents and even our abuela were all stuck in the past. He thought if he left that it would be better for everyone."

"And he told you all of that?"

"Yeah, but he didn't have to. I felt the same way for a long time."

"While you were gone."

"While I was gone."

"I'm glad you came back."

He didn't think she would answer, but just as he was beginning to drift into a light sleep, she said, "I am too."

They dozed for a few hours, then swapped off with Keme so he could get some sleep. Dylan could have stood watch on his own, but Akule had that vibrating energy about her again.

So they watched together.

And when the workers started arriving back in the camp, Keme joined them. No one spied Paco. Their position was too far away to be able to make out individuals. They had no way of knowing if Joshua had delivered the message or if he was going to turn them in to the guards.

Dylan thought you had to go with your instincts in this new postmodern world. Couldn't run a background check or scan someone's social media pages to see how their colors truly ran. Instinct was all a person had.

Of course, instincts could be wrong.

That was the rub.

Sometimes what you thought was instinct was actually wishful thinking. His instincts told him that Joshua was one of the good guys, and he did not for a minute think that was wishful thinking.

Few of the tent people hung around outside. Joshua had said that talking to one another was forbidden. On top of that, a stiff north wind continued to blow. Most of the people climbed into their tent, zipped it up, and didn't come out again. The guards made rounds then walked off toward the marina.

Darkness fell.

The temperature dropped.

The same guy they'd seen the night before began his rounds at ten p.m., again stopping on the south side of the building, lighting a cigarette, huddling out of the wind.

Dylan, Akule, and Keme crouched behind juniper bushes as they watched the bathroom where they'd first approached Joshua. The hands of Dylan's watch moved slowly toward one a.m., then one fifteen, one twenty.

And just when Dylan felt that perhaps it had been optimism and not instinct that caused them to trust Joshua...

Just when he began to worry that Akule might dart into the camp...

Just as hope began to fade to something darker...

There was movement in one of the tents. A tall man stepped out, followed by two children and a woman clutching a bundle. They moved away from where Dylan and Akule and Keme waited. As they crept toward the edge of the water, another person joined them. Dylan hoped it was Joshua.

Who else would it be?

His hand went to his revolver.

Still there. Still within reach.

All of the adults in the group carried a pack, though they didn't look heavy. Dylan doubted there was anything other than an extra set of clothes in them. No food. No weapons. They were fortunate if they got away with the clothes on their back. The group followed the shoreline north away from the tents, cut east, made their way to the bathroom, then crept behind it.

Akule waited until they approached the fence line, until they could hear a young voice ask, "Here, Dad?"

And then she was running toward them.

Keme was only steps behind.

Dylan heard an exclamation of surprise from Akule as the group came together. Saw her reach for the woman's bundle, then go down on her knees to hug her nephews. Keme embraced his son. Claire gathered the boys to her, and Joshua nudged the entire group toward Dylan who was keeping watch.

Keeping his firearm at the ready.

He might not have a family reunion in his future like the one playing out before him. But he'd do everything in his power to protect the one he'd just witnessed. There was something else too. These people huddled together on this dark, cold night felt like his own family.

Joshua, too, had held back—giving the family a moment of privacy.

And then they were creeping through the darkness, putting as much distance between their group and Camp Penn as was humanly possible, moving with urgency and fear and hope. It wasn't until they were on the far side of the college campus that Dylan heard and recognized the cry of an infant.

CHAPTER 13

Akule's heart was full.

Her brother, sister-in-law, nephews, and niece were here.

She was afraid it was a dream.

Afraid she would awaken and find herself back in her little apartment in Alpine, missing her mother and worrying over her brother.

The walk back to Mount Lebanon should have been terrible. Camp Penn goons might be following them. Vagrants like Stanley might try to attack. They were walking with two small children and an infant through a metroplex suburb that had been devastated. Akule was living through one of her worst nightmares.

Somehow the nightmare had shifted so that now it resembled one of her better dreams.

An answer to prayers she hadn't realized she'd uttered.

And even though she was tired, she wasn't exhausted. In fact, Akule felt exhilarated. They'd done what few thought they could. They'd found her brother.

Paco carried the infant. Pete insisted he could keep up on

his own. Keme carried little Danny. Akule led the group, her hand always hovering near her holster. Dylan and Joshua watched the back. No one followed. They saw no one else at all as they crept back to the small college campus, down the empty streets, across two creeks, behind deserted houses.

At least they looked deserted.

Were they?

Or were more families huddled there, wondering how to escape?

They approached Mount Lebanon from the back of the property, whistled twice, and were met by Duke.

"Good to see you." He led them to Morales's office, where they finally heard Paco's story.

"You've grown in number." Morales introduced herself to Paco and Claire, spoke softly to the children, gently touched the infant. Cocking her head in surprise at Joshua, she asked, "Grandfather?"

He smiled and said, "Just an old man no one sees."

"Joshua was left to clean bathrooms since he poses a threat to no one." Dylan shook his head in mock disgust. "I can't believe I fell for that act."

Joshua shrugged.

Morales sat in her chair, her attention fully on the group of refugees. "Will Martin send anyone after you?"

Joshua and Paco answered simultaneously. "No."

"How can you be so sure?"

"A couple of reasons." Joshua ran his hands along the arms of the chair as if he was surprised to find himself sitting in one. "He doesn't have as many guards as he once did. And he won't want to admit that anyone left."

"But people will notice you're all gone," Akule said.

"Maybe," Joshua admitted. "But there are several possible explanations for that. We could have died."

"The whole family?" Keme stared at the man in disbelief.

"It's happened—sadly, it has happened. Or, they might think that Paco and his family were transferred to a different camp. That's happened a few times too."

"There's more than one of those things?" Dylan fought to lower his voice. "You want to tell me how that's possible?"

"It's a long explanation, and I'd only be guessing. My point is, Martin won't come looking."

"Joshua, can you tell me how many guards there are?"

"Yes."

"Can you tell me where they're posted? And what the camp's weak points are?"

This time he merely nodded.

A smile played across Isabella's face. Akule thought the woman had a rescue attempt forming in her mind. She'd have liked to ride along for that. She wouldn't though. Her priority was to get the rest of her family back in Alpine, and that was exactly what she planned to do.

Joshua and Paco stayed behind to talk to Morales.

Claire, the children, Keme, Dylan, and Akule were walked over to the mess hall, where a decent dinner had been rustled up. Hot oatmeal. Granola bars. Juice. With full stomachs, both boys were soon nodding off in their chairs. Even the infant had fallen asleep.

The entire group reconvened in the same bunkhouse they'd used before. This time, a full row of beds was made up, a folded towel placed on top of each one, and another small bar of soap sat on the counter in the bathroom.

Joshua tried to leave, to give them time alone.

"Stay," Keme said. "You're one of us now. You made this possible. I owe you a debt that I don't know how to repay, but I will find a way."

The old man nodded and sat in one of the chairs they'd

pulled into a circle. There was no iron stove here. No chiminea. They all still wore their coats and hats and gloves. But Akule thought that was okay.

They were together. That's what mattered.

She could barely take her eyes off her brother, Claire, the boys, and the baby. If she blinked, would they disappear? Had her heart conjured them from thin air?

The first question out of Paco's mouth was, "How's mom?"

Which delivered a well-placed arrow to Akule's heart. She looked at her dad, who stared down at the infant in his arms. It was Dylan who rescued them.

"She died. We were in a battle with Marfa. I suppose that's a long story that can wait for another day. But you should know that she died defending Alpine. Defending her neighbors and her friends."

Akule found her voice. "And defending our family. Grandma and Grandpa are good. We're all still alive because of the people who fought for Alpine."

"Abuela?"

Keme shook his head. "She was one of the first to go. Her diabetes was difficult to control, and then one day she simply took a turn for the worse. It happened very quickly, but we were able to be there with her when she passed from this life to the next."

Paco nodded as if that made sense.

Akule realized this must be a lot of information to receive all at once. Just as they had been worried about Paco and his family, he had been concerned about them.

She tried to think of something that would lighten the mood and then her eyes fell on the bundle in Keme's arms. "Tell us about my niece. Tell us about Lucinda."

Claire was blonde, slender, and Anglo.

She was the very opposite of Paco who was dark-skinned like Akule, huskier, with lighter hair like their mom's.

They'd managed to produce the most beautiful family. Looking at them caused Akule's throat to ache. She'd tried not to think about the future, tried to ignore everything but each day's challenges. Looking at her two nephews and her niece, she understood that would have to change.

She needed to actively prepare for the days and years to come.

Claire reached for Paco's hand, squeezed it, and glanced over at her two sons who were asleep together in one bed. Then she turned a loving gaze on her daughter, nestled in her grandfather's arms. "We found out I was pregnant in the spring, well before June 6th. Our plan was to tell you over the July 4th holiday. We wanted to do it in person. That didn't happen."

They waited, didn't rush her. Akule understood that Claire needed to tell this in her own way.

"She was born in November and we both knew that we wanted to name her after Lucy. She has her smile."

Little Lucy woke and let out a husky cry.

Keme quickly passed the babe to Claire and everyone laughed. "It's been a while since I cared for a crying infant."

Paco stared at them, unashamedly brushing the tears from his face. "I can't believe you're here."

"Tell us about the camp." Keme sat back in his chair. "Why did you go there? Why didn't you come home when everything went dark?"

"Claire was pregnant. The highways were jammed. Everything we heard indicated that traveling would be too dangerous."

"We talked about it," Claire said. "The government was still broadcasting at that point. Telling everyone to shelter in place. Saying that the situation—that's what they called it —*the situation* . . ."

Anger briefly flashed across Claire's face, replaced quickly with an exhaustion that Akule understood very well.

Paco took up the story. "They said *the situation* was being dealt with. But after the first week, we knew that wasn't true. A few neighbors stayed—two more days, maybe three. Then the explosions downtown started. That scared people. They fled, even when they had no idea where they were going."

"It's true." Joshua had been silent, but now he sat forward, elbows on his knees. "I can only imagine what it was like in a remote place like Alpine. Here in the metroplex lack of information wasn't the problem. If anything, there was too much of it. There was simply no way to tell what was the truth and what wasn't. That frightened people as much as anything else."

"What about the police?" Akule was thinking of Tanda, of how hard her aunt had worked to maintain some semblance of law and order.

Paco shook his head. "They tried. I guess. Most of them also had families to care for, and by the second week, attacks were coming from all sides. It all fell apart pretty quickly."

"Then someone broke in and stole most of our food."

"They must have been watching the house. We would go out and scavenge for maybe an hour every day. I didn't want to leave Claire alone—"

"We thought staying together was the most important thing."

"One day we returned home to find all of our supplies gone." Paco scrubbed a hand over his face. "I've replayed it in my mind a hundred times—what we might have done differently, where else we could have gone, how we could have made it home."

"The camp seemed our only alternative."

"At first it wasn't so bad."

"Because at first Martin wasn't the one in charge." Joshua leaned back, hands behind his head, fingers intertwined. "In those early days, it was just some campers who had been at the park when the satellites fell."

"So you know about that?" Akule resisted the urge to look up, to stare at the ceiling and beyond.

"Yeah. That got around pretty early on, and then there was the crash of a few of them in the metroplex. Didn't take long for word to travel as to what it was, though why..."

As one, they fell silent.

"So there were a few campers, then people heard it was a safe place and the group grew. A man named Garner was in charge then. Paco and Claire, I think that's when you first arrived."

They nodded in agreement.

"What happened to him?" Dylan asked.

"Martin killed him. After that, things went downhill quickly."

"Okay. We could do this all night." Keme fought a yawn. "But we'll have lots of time to catch up when we're on the road. We have two, maybe three hours before daylight. Let's try to grab some sleep, and in the morning we'll figure out our next step."

Akule knew he was right.

She didn't want to sleep though.

She wanted to watch over her family.

She wanted to stand guard.

It was Dylan who assured her that Milo and Duke would take care of that.

"Do you think they're it? That Morales and Milo and Duke are the only ones here?"

"I do not. I think they're the only ones we've met. Morales is pretty careful. Gotta respect her for that."

"Yeah." Akule lay down on her cot. Dylan sleeping to her right. Claire to her left. Then she remembered what was in her backpack. She sat up, rummaged through it, found the packet of letters, and walked over to Paco's cot.

Sitting on the floor, she waited until he raised his eyes to hers, then she put the letters in his hand. "From mom."

Paco ran a finger over the piece of ribbon holding the slim packet of letters together.

"She wrote one a week, from June 6th until she died. Said she'd hand them to you when you got home, so you'd know that she'd been thinking of you."

Tears slipped down Paco's cheeks. He leaned forward, pulled her into a hug, and she threw her arms around him.

Silently, she made her way back to her cot, closed her eyes, and dreamed of home.

Morales could provide transportation out of the metroplex, maybe as far as Glen Rose. Once there, Keme knew they'd have to make a decision about which route to take. I-20 was the northernmost route, but apparently it wasn't an option.

"Impassable," was all Morales would say.

The safest route was also the most rural one—south then west, along the 281/190. But they needed to pick up the horses which meant going through Brownwood, then south on 67.

"For now, let's just get you to Glen Rose." Morales walked to where Akule stood waiting, pulled a red bandana from her pocket, and tied it around Akule's neck. Then she tied a blue one around Keme's neck and a white one around Paco's. "This will tell people that you're on the right side of things."

"Hope none of the bad guys are walking around sporting red, white, and blue bandanas." Dylan laughed, but clearly the idea made him nervous.

"It's unlikely they would have all three. We found boxes of these a few months ago. It's better than a note. A note can be intercepted and put people at risk. A bandana. . ." She shrugged. "It's just a bandana."

"What will you do when you run out?" Keme asked.

"Choose a different signal. It's a good idea to do that periodically anyway."

Morales, Duke, and Milo saw them out to a waiting Chevy S-10 truck that had seen better days. It had gas though—somehow. It ran, which was really all they needed. Keme, his family, Dylan, and Joshua all piled into the bed of the truck. Someone had found another set of clothes for Joshua. Not new, but not as ragged as the ones he'd been wearing. Claire and the children sat up against the back of the cab, huddled down and covered with blankets.

As Keme watched Camp Lebanon fade into the distance, he wondered at the fact that they had found it and connected with these good people. He kept stumbling over the realization that those things had all occurred through a low-life, not-quite-recovered junkie named Stanley. You never knew, in this world, who would be the person to help you through or around or over the next obstacle. Stanley hadn't done that, but he'd led them to the people who had.

It was only sixty miles from Cedar Hill to Glen Rose. Before June 6th it would have been a one-hour trip, but it took them most of the next two days to cross that distance. They walked, rode in the back of more pickup trucks, and for the final fifteen miles hitched a ride with a small RV caravan.

All were people that Morales vouched for and trusted.

All were people sporting bandanas.

Keme thought that once in Glen Rose they might head to the state park, a place he'd taken Paco and Akule when they were young—known for the dinosaur tracks discovered when the water level was low in the Paluxy River. They didn't make it quite that far. The RV people had let them off on the northeast side of town. "Follow this road south to the bend in the river. You'll find a group of people at Big Rocks Park. They're Morales's people. We wish you Godspeed."

And then they were gone. Five RVs, each filled with two to three families, carefully watching the gas gauge and praying they had enough to reach a safe destination. Two of the families had heard about a new community north of Lake Granbury. They were betting all they had on it being there and allowing them inside.

The clouds pressed low.

Rain or snow?

Keme hoped that whichever it was, it would pass through quickly.

They walked by several signs that proclaimed Glen Rose to be

Dinosaur Capital of Texas

"Remember the dinosaur tracks?" Paco teased his sister.

"You told me that one was going to sneak up on me in my sleep and eat me for a snack."

"And you believed me."

"How can a dinosaur sneak up on someone?" Pete asked.

"Good question, son."

They'd kept to their pattern of the night before. Akule led the group. Dylan and Joshua watched the back. Keme stayed in the middle with Paco and his family.

He had the feeling they were being watched. When they

were half a mile from the river, two men and a woman stepped out from behind two tankers that had been placed across the road. Keme was close enough to see the red, white, and blue bandanas.

"What's your business?" The woman asked.

"Seeking sanctuary." Those were the words Morales told them to use.

Perhaps it was the fact that they had children with them. Or maybe because Little Lucy picked that moment to let out a lusty cry. Marauders probably wouldn't be carrying an infant. Most likely it was the bandanas or the words that guaranteed refuge. Regardless of the reason, the taller of the two men waved them through. "Let's get you to the river."

Big Rocks Park was exactly that—a park that had been formed around large sedimentary rocks. Keme realized those rocks would provide useful cover in the case of an attack. Trees shaded the banks of the river. A sandy area was adjacent to a small dam on one end of the park. There was also a public restroom and several picnic tables.

It was an ingenious place to house a refugee site.

The river would supply all the water they needed.

The rocks provided a barrier.

"In the summer some folks camp out and sleep in their tents," the woman explained. "Sleeping arrangements at the center are adequate but a bit crowded. It's a relief to have a little space as well as privacy. During the winter though, we all stay down at the retreat center."

The retreat center reminded Keme of Mount Lebanon, though it was smaller. How many summer camps, retreat centers, and wellness resorts were there in Texas? In the U.S.? In the world? And how many of them now housed displaced, homeless, frightened citizens?

But the people they passed didn't look frightened.

"How big is this place?" Keme asked.

"Eighty acres. I'm Kate, by the way. Kate Wilson."

"Good to meet you, Kate."

"We realized pretty early on that this would be the place to make our stand."

"Not the state park?"

"There's another group there, but this location had more of what we anticipated needing."

A family with three children walked across a grassy area.

Two teenaged boys tossed a football.

Keme had the strange feeling of having stepped into a parallel universe, one untouched by the tragedies of the last six months.

"Bet that swimming pool comes in handy," Akule said.

Kate laughed. "We'll think of something to do with that. One of the reasons we chose this spot was the housing—three cabins, two lodges, what was employee accommodations, plus various other buildings. And the property includes a high point which is a good place to keep watch."

"How long has this facility been here?" Akule asked.

"Since 1939." Kate led them into the Ellis Education Building, down a hall, and to what looked like an open library. Two of the walls were covered with floor-to-ceiling shelves filled with books. The other two sides of the room were open to the juncture of two halls. Armchairs and side tables finished out the space.

There wasn't any electricity, but large skylights provided plenty of light.

Pete bounced from one foot to another. "Can we look at the books, Mom?"

Claire looked like Keme felt, as if she'd stepped into Alice's Wonderland. She opened her mouth to answer him but didn't seem to know what to say.

"You're welcome to read our books, son. It's why we have them." A trim woman with short gray hair and perfect posture joined them.

With her was a completely bald man who was over six feet tall and wore suspenders. He smiled broadly at Pete and Danny. "Let me show you the kids' section. . . if your mom says it's okay." He wiggled his eyebrows at Pete and Danny, then glanced at Claire.

"Yeah. Sure. Just be careful with the books."

"My name is Beverly Skinner," the woman said. "Let's sit. I'm sure you all are exhausted. Would you like some coffee?"

"If that's a joke, it's a cruel one." Joshua dropped his pack on the floor and shook her hand, as did the rest of the group.

"No joke. We make it weak so the supplies we have will last longer, but it's hot and we have a little sugar and milk."

Ten minutes later they were all seated, clutching mugs of coffee, trying to decide which of a dozen questions to answer first.

Kate saved them from the mental exercise. "Bill worked at the Comanche Nuclear Power Plant, which is nine miles north of here on Squaw Creek Reservoir. The plant shut down in the early morning hours of June 6th. Thirteen hundred employees were sent home. Someone knew the grid was about to go down, and they expected it to stay down."

Keme glanced over at Bill, who was sitting on the floor reading a book about dinosaurs to Pete and Danny. "Bill warned everyone?"

"He didn't have to. Everyone in Glen Rose knew about the plant closing before the employees made it home. We still had cell phones then. Texts were flying faster than bullets at the Alamo."

"I remember when the nuclear plant was built," Joshua said. "Kinda controversial."

"Construction began in 1974. A lot of people in the area supported the building of it, and some even approved of the 2008 request to expand the nuclear plant. After all, it provided a lot of jobs."

"But not everyone supported it." Joshua rubbed at his jaw. "Wasn't there something in the news about protests?"

"Both environmental and anti-nuclear organizations were opposed to the project, and for a variety of reasons that expansion never happened. The plant continued to operate though. And some people in the area remained concerned about the possible dangers should an accident occur. Years ago, the citizens of Glen Rose put an emergency disaster plan in place. That came in handy on June 6th."

"The government initiated the disaster plan?" Claire was holding her infant close, as if she needed to protect her from some yet unforeseen danger.

"No. They didn't. And that was concerning in and of itself. We knew the shutdown wasn't for scheduled maintenance, and sending everyone home didn't make sense. Bill initiated the emergency plan. He was the head of the disaster management board at that point. I was the liaison with the regional Red Cross Unit."

"Wow." Dylan gazed around the room. "Just, wow. I don't think we've come across a place that's weathered June 6th better than Alpine, but this place just might have."

"This place. . ." She waved a hand to encompass the room, building, and entire campus. "This was our fallback position in case of such an emergency. We even had medical supplies and food stored here."

"And books." Akule nodded toward the tall shelves.

"We don't have everything we want, but—for now—we have everything we need."

"And you haven't been attacked?" Keme sat back and

sipped his coffee. Coffee. It had been four months since he'd tasted the stuff. It was better than he remembered. Richer.

"A few groups have tried. I think word spread quickly that we would defend this place and these people. In addition, we're not on the main road. The kind of thugs you're talking about are lazy, in my opinion. They want easy targets. Soft targets. We are neither of those things."

Dinosaur sounds came from where the boys were still reading with Bill. The man looked up, met Keme's gaze, and nodded once.

Keme realized that Morales was right.

These were trustworthy people.

"Now let's talk about you," Beverly said. "Tell me what you need and how we can help."

CHAPTER 14

Tell me what you need.

Dylan hadn't heard those words in quite some time. Few people were offering help these days. Though Morales had. Franklin had. Stella and Jimbo Bright had.

There were still good people in the world.

That was something Dylan tended to forget.

Keme explained that they were headed home—headed to Alpine. That they'd rescued Paco and his family from a camp next to Joe Pool Lake. That they'd known they would be traveling with two children, but they hadn't known about Little Lucy.

"It's even more complicated than that," Dylan said. "We need to go back through San Angelo. We need to pick up our horses."

Beverly stood and walked over to a map that had been pinned to the wall. "Before June 6th, the shortest route from here to Alpine was through San Angelo. Truckers tended to go I-20, which angles you farther north but allowed for higher speeds on better roads. That's not an option for us at this point."

"Because of robbers?" Joshua asked. "Highwaymen?"

She smiled at the old term. "Yes, but also government sweeps."

"We still don't understand that," Keme admitted. "Why are they bothering to gather up citizens?"

"Depends who you're talking to. I've spoken to men and women running those transports. They remain convinced that they're helping people, getting them into safe zones."

"We heard a different story," Akule said. "We heard there's a camp, north of Guadalupe Mountains National Park, that's a tent city. There's a fence around it and people aren't allowed out. We heard they're gathering folks who would be needed for a new community—doctors, engineers, teachers. They're taking them whether they want to go or not."

Beverly cocked her head. "I haven't heard that one yet. Regardless of the reason, if your goal is Alpine that's not the direction you want to travel."

"So we go through San Angelo. That's where we need to collect the horses anyway."

Instead of agreeing, Beverly studied the map, frowning at it. Finally she turned to the group. "You are, of course, free to leave any time you want. You've proven yourselves resourceful. You've managed to get this far. You could make it home."

Dylan's gaze flicked to the baby, to the two small boys. Would they make it? How?

"If you can give me a little time—maybe twenty-four hours—I'll see what I can come up with as far as transporting you through the underground network. I'm not promising anything." She held up a hand as if she could stop their hopes from rising. "But I'll try."

They were escorted to a gymnasium where cots were set up

across the floor. The room had only a few other families in it, but Dylan could imagine what it must have looked like initially, how full it must have been.

Claire sank onto a cot and began nursing the baby.

A worker came over, explained where the bathrooms were and what time dinner would be served, then handed a bucket of toys to the boys. They sank down on the rug between two cots and proceeded to pull out trucks and Matchbox cars and plastic animals.

"We passed a group of people on the porch of one of those cabins." Keme nodded to the east. "Think I'll head over and see what they know."

"I'll go with you," Joshua said.

Dylan looked at Akule. "Want to go walk by the river?"

"I do, but. . ." She glanced at Claire, who waved her away. "We'll be fine."

Claire smiled at her boys. Danny was already rubbing his eyes, and Pete was lying on his stomach, placing cars in a line.

"All right," Akule said. "To the river it is, cowboy."

They walked to the dam. The sun came out. They sat on a picnic table. Tossed around their options—which were few. Then started back toward the main cluster of buildings, passing a group of people their age in the process.

There were probably a dozen, of various ethnicities, and aged sixteen to young twenties, if Dylan were to guess. He was terrible at guessing ages, so he could have been way off. Some were obviously from the city—they were talking about cars, movies, and professional sports teams. Others were from small towns. They were reminiscing about big trucks, mudding, rodeos, even fishing.

"Well, hell, Travis. You could throw a rock and hit the Paluxy. Go on out there and catch us some dinner."

"Those fish aren't biting and you know it. But I'm talking about gulf fishing. Tarpon and speckled trout and black drum."

"Shrimp."

"Hush puppies."

"French fries."

The group fell silent, until Travis, the would-be coastal fisherman, asked Akule and Dylan where they were from. They explained about riding from Alpine, losing their horses to the group in San Angelo, continuing on to the metroplex, and finding Paco.

"You're lucky you made it out of Dallas," Travis said. "I heard if you're caught breaking curfew they assign you to a work crew."

"I heard they're shipping people to a new community in Oklahoma." This from a girl with chopped hair and freckles.

The group fell silent again as they tried to imagine what a new community might look like. Finally Akule said, "I'm not going on a work crew, and I'm not going to Oklahoma. I'm going home."

And then she stalked off.

"It's been a tough few weeks," Dylan explained. "Hope y'all get wherever you're going."

"Yeah, you too, man."

He had to jog to catch up with her.

"You okay?"

Instead of answering she trudged on, silently. She didn't tell him to leave, so he figured it couldn't hurt to go with her. She didn't slow until she'd passed the retreat center and was back among the large rocks that bordered the river. Finally, she found one five feet high sitting in a splash of sunlight, scrambled up to the top, and pulled her knees to her chest.

He joined her.

He didn't speak because he had no idea what to say.

A few minutes passed. He didn't rush her. He didn't have anywhere to be. He realized, in a sudden moment of clarity, that if the world were as it was before, he'd still want to be where he was at this moment—sitting beside Akule. Maybe with a fresh pizza and a beer, but still sitting beside Akule.

Her forehead pressed to her knees, she began to speak. Her voice was muffled, and he had to lean in to hear her.

"What if we can't do it? What if we can't make it? What if Pete and Danny and Little Lucy were better off in that terrible camp?"

She didn't look up, but he knew she was waiting for an answer.

"We can. We will. And they weren't."

Now she turned her head to the side, cheek pressed against her knees, and studied him. "Are you always this optimistic?"

He wanted to put his arms around her, but Akule reminded him of a young doe—skittish, wary, easily startled. Instead of risking a move that might be rebuffed, he flashed her a smile.

She rolled her eyes, wiped the tears off her cheeks, and sat up straighter. "This sucks."

"Yup."

"Sorry you came along?"

"Nope."

They sat there, watching the sun dip toward the horizon, then made their way back to the gymnasium. Dinner was some kind of vegetable soup with a hard piece of bread on the side.

"Tack," Joshua explained.

"How do you know that?"

"Oh, I know things. Don't try eating it until it's had a chance to soften. You'll break a tooth, and I doubt there's a dentist nearby." Joshua dropped his bread into his soup, wiggled his eyebrows, and then swallowed a big spoonful of the broth.

Keme and Paco had learned that most families stayed one night at the retreat center, maybe two. Everyone they had talked to was traveling on. Everyone had a destination in mind, a place they hoped would be better and permanent.

Claire had spoken to two of the other moms. One had been in a camp where the flu had spread like wildfire. “People dying of the flu. Can you imagine?”

“The Spanish flu killed one-third of the world’s population.” Joshua’s voice was soft, factual, but his eyes drifted to the windows and the world beyond. “We’ve since developed some immunity to influenza viruses, but an outbreak when people are living in these conditions without medical care...well, it could be devastating.”

Dylan stared at Joshua.

The entire group had stopped eating and was staring at Joshua, except for the boys who were trying to crumble their *tack* against the table top.

Keme leaned close to Dylan and in a stage whisper said, “He really does know things.”

“Yeah, but do we want to know what he knows?”

Joshua laughed and the tension around the little group dissipated a fraction. Still there. Still a constant undercurrent. But tinged less with fear, if that was possible. Dylan didn’t think you could make it in this world if you allowed yourself to be consumed by fear. It would be too exhausting.

They ate. Surprisingly the tack did soften, and it at least added some bulk to the soup. They spoke about their possible routes home, tossed around what they would do first when they reached Alpine. And Dylan knew they would reach Alpine. One way or another, they’d get there.

The boys nearly nodded off in their soup bowls. Paco carried Pete, Keme carried Danny, and Claire carried little Lucy. They all checked their packs, laid out what they’d need in the morning, settled onto their cots. But Dylan couldn't sleep. He tossed left, then right. Punched his pillow. Even pulled the single blanket over his head. Nothing worked. He'd slept better on the ground between Sanderson and San Angelo.

He felt keyed up. Felt as if something was coming but since he didn't know what it was he had no idea how to defend against it.

He slipped from his cot, grabbed his sleeping bag, and walked out to the foyer of the gym, where a shaft of moonlight spilled through the glass walls. He'd been there maybe twenty minutes when Akule showed up, her sleeping bag under her arm, a deck of Uno cards in her hands.

She held them out.

He shuffled.

They played until well past midnight. Until the moon was high and their eyes were stinging from lack of sleep. They didn't bother going back to their cots but simply pulled their sleeping bags around them, used chair cushions for pillows, and lay down side by side.

After a few minutes, the fears that hounded them quieted enough that they could slip into much-needed sleep. Dylan's last thought was that he didn't know how this was going to end, but he did know that he would be at Akule's side until they were back in Alpine.

Until they were home.

AKULE WOKE with a crick in her neck. Still, she felt better than she had the day before. Felt oddly refreshed and ready to move forward. The entire group was finally ushered into Beverly Skinner's office just before lunch. The office didn't look that different from the library. Fewer books. More maps on the wall.

She didn't waste any time. "The only way that I see this working is if you split your group in half."

"No," Keme said.

But Akule leaned forward. "Tell us more."

"Let's start with the route to San Angelo, which is the most problematic. I can get you to Brownwood, possibly Santa Anna. From there you would have to walk to Ballinger."

"Not that far," Dylan said.

"Thirty miles, at least." Beverly's eyes flicked to the boys who were once again sitting on the floor, cross-legged, this time playing with puzzles they'd found in a plastic crate. "Sixty miles if you have to walk from Brownwood to Ballinger, which is a possibility."

"And then?"

"We have someone in Ballinger who can get you to the edge of San Angelo. But he can only take three. He's adamant that three is the limit. He's tried larger groups. It didn't end well."

"We'll find another way," Keme said.

"If we did split up, how would the other group get home?" Joshua was staring intently at the map on the wall behind Beverly's desk.

It wasn't a map of Texas. It was a world map. Akule thought it probably had been there before June 6th. No one needed a world map anymore. Maybe Beverly left it there to remind herself of the bigger picture. That there was more than Glen Rose, Texas. There was a whole world out there, and they were all trying to solve the same problems.

They were all trying to find a way to exist.

Akule wasn't sure what group Joshua saw himself in, but she couldn't imagine him walking thirty to sixty miles. Yes, he was a far cry from the old man they'd first spied shuffling toward the camp bathrooms, but he still had to be in his sixties, possibly seventies.

"That's actually my good news. We take the other group this way. . . south." Her fingers traced from Glen Rose to Goldthwaite, San Saba, Llano. "All the way to Junction, then we skirt south and west. County roads, private roads, farms. We have a group going to the border near Candelaria. You can ride with them."

"All of us?"

"No. Half—maybe. If the other half decides not to go to San Angelo, to give up on retrieving your horses, they'd still need to wait here until the next transport goes through. Could be a few weeks. Could be longer."

Keme stood, paced the room.

Paco had no problem deciding. "We split up then. I'll go south."

"No, you need to stay with your wife and children." Keme turned back toward them, arms crossed, a scowl etched on his face.

Beverly held up a hand. "This is a personal discussion. Take a few hours, then let me know what you decide."

Everyone was silent on the walk back to the gymnasium. One of the workers had left a few books on the small camp table. The boys each grabbed a book, jumped onto their shared cot, and were immediately immersed in a world filled with wild beasts—Tyrannosaurus and Torosaurus and Deinonychus. Claire placed a sleeping Lucy on her cot, then surrounded the baby with pillows.

The adults had barely pulled their chairs into a circle when everyone started talking at once.

Keme held up his hand in a stop signal. "One at a time."

Which, Akule realized, was the Alpine way. State your

opinion. Explain your reasons. Come to a consensus. Move forward.

Claire started. "Obviously the children and I need to take the southern route, and not only because we can't walk it. We could, I think. But we would slow you down. And if the weather were to turn..."

"We won't risk that," Paco agreed. "But I feel torn. Feel I should be with you and the kids, and also feel that I should help get the horses back. I'm the reason you lost them."

"You're not," Dylan said. "We lost them because of an asshole named Douglas Perkins."

"We could leave them," Keme pointed out. "We could leave the horses and the mule."

"Yes, we could." Akule didn't like the idea at all, but she had to admit it was an option. "Why should we though? If we don't have to? Dylan and I can go that way. Walking thirty miles won't be a problem. Even sixty wouldn't be that difficult. We could make twenty miles a day—that's a five-day walk at most. We'd still make it to San Angelo before our thirty days are up."

Her father studied her. She appreciated the fact that he didn't question her ability. Sometime since leaving Alpine, he'd accepted that she was a capable adult. "Remember, you have to take Perkins something. That was part of the deal."

"Yeah, I remember. And we'll find something. We'll trade for something along the way."

"Keme, you should go with Paco. You've been separated long enough. See them home. See them safely home." Joshua's smile spread across his face. "I can keep up with Dylan and Akule."

Could he?

Really?

Akule wasn't so sure, but she had to admit that she

admired his spirit. Everyone stopped talking—stared at their hands, the floor, the ceiling, and finally one another. Trying to envision this thing they were about to attempt. Carefully considering the decisions they were making.

Finally Dylan broke the silence. "Three's always better than two."

Akule thought it was exactly what he'd said to her in Alpine. She hadn't wanted him to come with them then. She didn't want Joshua to come with them now. But she'd been wrong before, and perhaps this time she was wrong as well.

It was decided.

Three was always better than two.

Akule, Dylan, and Joshua would go to San Angelo.

Keme, Paco, Claire, and the children would take the southern route and hopefully beat them home.

CHAPTER 15

Keme watched Akule, Dylan, and Joshua climb into the bed of a dilapidated pickup truck the next morning. A mother and two children were crammed into the cab next to the driver. Another family of six sat in the bed of the pickup. The day was sunny, unseasonably warm. In typical Texas weather fashion, it felt like early spring.

It was not early spring.

It was mid-January and winter wasn't done with them yet.

Keme had shook Joshua's hand, gave Dylan a clumsy pat on the shoulder, and pulled his daughter close to his heart. He had the foreboding thought that he'd found one child only to lose another, but he pushed that thought away.

They weren't children. They were adults.

More importantly, he couldn't allow himself to indulge such fears. He wasn't one who thought saying a thing could make it so. But he knew, firsthand, that giving fear a foothold only served to weaken every single thing you tried to do.

Keme stood there waving until the truck was out of sight.

"She'll be okay, Dad." Paco swung Danny up and onto his

shoulders. The little boy giggled, reached over and patted his grandfather's head.

"You're right," Keme said. "Akule has adjusted faster than most."

"My little sister is all grown up."

Keme didn't know if Paco was trying to offer comfort or convince himself. He did know the sure cure for their current worries was to stay busy. "Think I'll go through our supplies one more time, then take a look at the left-and-take room."

Akule had taken one-third of the food, half of the ammo, and all of the items left to trade. He'd tried to convince her to take more of the food and all of the ammo, but in her typical way, she shook her head and resolutely refused.

Paco took the children to the playground while Claire and Keme went through the things that had been left by others. Keme didn't know his daughter-in-law well. Had always wondered what Paco saw in her. She had seemed so different from them. She was from the city, refined, wealthy, and Anglo.

"Have you spoken with your parents, Claire?"

"They both died."

He froze, studied her, and finally offered, "I'm sorry."

"I am too, but..." She shook her head as she sat on the floor of the storage room and pulled a box of children's clothes toward her. "This world would have been very difficult for them to navigate."

He must have looked surprised, because she immediately explained, "My dad traded stocks for a living. He had cardiovascular disease, which was held in check with medication. Without the medication, his life would have been hell."

"Were you there when he passed?" Keme was thinking of Abuela. Of sitting with her as a breeze came through the window. Tanda, his parents, Akule, Lucy, Doc Miles. . . they'd held vigil. They'd stayed with her as she passed from this life to the next.

"I wasn't with him. They only lived a block away from us. I went by there every day. The fourth day after the event, I showed up and my mom was sitting by his bed, holding his hand." Claire tucked a strand of blonde hair behind her ear.

Keme noticed her hand was shaking. When she met his gaze, her eyes were shiny with tears.

"We moved her in with us then, but her diabetes was already spiraling out of control and her will was broken. She passed a few days later."

"I'm so very sorry."

"Thank you, Keme." She cocked her head and seemed to consider her words before adding, "I'm sorry about Lucy. She was a very special woman."

He didn't know how to answer that, how to speak around the lump in his throat, so he didn't try.

This wasn't the first left-and-take room he'd seen. When a population became mobile, such things became the norm. They'd had one at Alpine for a time, though few visitors came through anymore. He'd also seen one at the Mount Lebanon encampment, but he hadn't had time to visit it. Basically, it was a place to put all the shit that people thought of as important before June 6th. As they began to walk, to make their way through this new landscape, they discarded things. . . mostly useless things. But occasionally what was no longer important to one person was a real find for someone else.

Hence, the name left-and-take room.

They pawed through the boxes filled with things that no one needed—cell phone chargers, e-readers, DVDs, car fobs, remote-controlled toys, handheld gaming systems, headphones. All fragments of a life left behind.

He picked up a deodorant stick and showed it to Claire. "Want it?"

"Sure do. That son of yours has some serious body odor, especially in the summer."

She laughed, and he marveled at that. This woman had been through a terrifying event, lost both her parents, and was now traveling across Texas with her three small children and a father-in-law she barely knew. Claire Lopez was made of tough stuff.

He pocketed a small, high-powered flashlight. One of the Sul Ross students had worked out how to adapt a solar charger originally intended for phones. They could now use it to recharge batteries, though how long the batteries would continue to recharge was anyone's guess. Still, the flashlight was small and might prove useful.

Claire picked out two outfits for baby Lucy.

"There are more infant clothes in this box," he said.

"I brought some with us, though she'll outgrow them quickly. Two is enough. Someone else might need those."

The last thing he found was an emergency whistle threaded onto a bright orange cord. Tanda would definitely want that. She was always looking for ways to help the older people in their town feel safe. She worried about them falling down and not having a Life Alert button or a cell phone to call 9-1-1. The emergency whistle would be better than nothing.

Bill and Beverly found them an hour later. The entire group ate lunch at one of the tables placed on the far side of the gymnasium. It was a simple meal—canned chili, crackers, cheese. It wasn't much, but it would do and Keme found himself grateful that Morales had directed them to this place and these people.

"We want to update you on your transport," Bill said, sitting across from them.

Apparently, Beverly dealt with the day-to-day issues of the camp. Bill handled moving people from one location to another. “As Beverly mentioned to you, there’s a truck headed down to the border.”

“Yes.” Keme pushed his plate away, crossed his arms on the table, looked at Bill and then at Beverly. “You said we’d go through Goldthwaite, San Saba, Llano.”

“Correct.”

“It’s not the quickest route to the border.”

“But it’s the safest,” Beverly assured him.

“You’ll be leaving at sundown, riding in a cattle truck, and there are twenty-two of you going. Ages range from very young —” Bill’s gaze flicked to Little Lucy and he smiled. “To the elderly.”

“Is there a danger that we’ll be stopped?” Paco asked.

“There is. Though we haven’t had that happen in the last few weeks. Most folks are hunkered down, probably waiting out winter. Government sweeps have become few and far between.” Bill pulled a map out of his shirt pocket and spread it on the table. “See the direction you’re going? South-southwest. Highway 281 to 16 to 29. I’m not going to lie to you. It’s going to be unpleasant riding in a cattle trailer that far.”

“We can handle unpleasant,” Claire assured him.

“Good. I’m glad to hear that. Some folks—they kind of assume we’re running an Uber here. It’s not quite that simple.”

Beverly drummed her fingertips against the table. “Antoine will be your driver. This will be his fourteenth trip. He knows what to avoid and how to deal with anyone he can’t outrun.”

“Is he armed?” Keme asked.

“He is, as I know you are. That’s one reason I’m telling you this. Most of the other folks are families, Mr. Lopez. They are tired, scared, and want to go home. They’ve been sheltering in place since June 6th. They do not have your experience or your. . .” Here she smiled slightly. “Or your skills.”

Keme had assured her that he was experienced with a handgun, that he’d helped to ride the perimeter in Alpine, that he’d fought in the battle with Marfa.

“Thomas will be riding shotgun. This is his first trip.” Bill shrugged. “Young kid—nineteen, if you can believe it. But he wants to go. He wants to learn how to do this, and we don’t have an overabundance of volunteers.”

“You said this will be Antoine’s fourteenth trip.” Paco said. “That’s a lot. If you don’t mind my asking, what’s his motivation? Why does he keep doing it?”

“His family was killed, trying to walk to El Paso.”

Keme had been studying the map, but at the mention of El Paso his head jerked up. “We had a family come from there. The man, Cade, was a doctor in the barrio. It sounds as if it was a pretty bad situation three months ago. I can’t imagine what it’s like now.”

“Same thing that we’ve heard. But this was in the early days. No one knew what was happening. Folks reacted instinctively, and Antoine’s parents wanted to go back to El Paso, back to family. They were ambushed. Only Antoine survived.”

Bill took up the story. “His way of making those people pay, of exacting retribution, is by seeing that other people do make it home. Trust me. You’re in good hands.”

Which seemed to be all that needed to be said.

They all stood and shook hands. Paco thanked them for providing sanctuary as well as transportation. Imitating their dad, Pete and then Danny walked over to Beverly and Bill, shook hands, and said, “Thank you, ma’am. Thanks, mister.” It occurred to Keme, not for the first time, that this new world, this post-modern, apocalyptic place, would be the world that Pete and Danny and Lucy grew up in.

What was it his wife used to say? Normal is a setting on the dryer. His grandchildren would have a new normal. They would adapt because they wouldn't remember what came before.

Keme was determined that they would grow up, not on the road lurching from town to town, but in Alpine surrounded by friends, neighbors, and what family they had left.

IT OCCURRED to Dylan that he would gladly give his right arm for a horse. Maybe not the whole arm. Not a hand. A pinky. He'd definitely be willing to part with a pinky.

The truck was old. The paint peeling. The engine sputtered whenever they accelerated. Dylan didn't know if it was the gasoline beginning to break down or if the vehicle needed a tune-up. Either way, he doubted it would get them across half of Texas.

The drive to Stephenville took almost three hours. Three hours to go sixty miles. It was enough to make a cowboy throw down his Stetson and stomp on it. Dylan was not going to throw his Stetson on the ground. As far as he knew, Stetson wouldn't be making any new hats for the foreseeable future.

His frustration grew steadily throughout the morning. To begin with they detoured half a dozen times around lines of abandoned cars. Then when the road was finally clear, when he thought they'd make real progress, they needed to reroute because a bridge had been blown up. Why would anyone blow up a bridge in rural Texas? Finally, they hit open road—only to have to stop for a scraggly herd of stray cows.

"I wouldn't mind a medium rare steak right now," he'd joked.

Joshua had laughed. Akule gave him the somber look that said *quit jacking around* as plainly as any words could.

The other two families had been dropped off on a county road east of Stephenville. Joshua climbed into the cab next to Kari Ann, their driver, leaving Akule and Dylan in the bed of the truck.

"I was hoping to actually see Stephenville not just drive around it," Dylan admitted.

"Why?"

"See what it's like."

"I suppose it's the same as any place else. Filled with people struggling to get by."

Kari Ann skirted around the town, keeping to county roads. No one bothered them, though twice Dylan saw riders who were probably on patrol and once he saw a group of folks working in a field. He couldn't imagine what they were doing in a field in January, but then he wasn't exactly up to date on farming techniques in this part of Texas.

"How old do you think she is?" Dylan asked.

"Kari Ann?"

"Yeah."

"I don't know. Why does it matter?"

"Doesn't. I was just thinking that she seems kind of young to be leading families through the underground."

"She probably thinks we're young to be rescuing horses from a survivalist compound."

"Point taken."

It wasn't that Dylan didn't trust the woman. She certainly knew her way around the backroads of Texas. It was more that he couldn't get over the thought that she probably wasn't old enough to order a glass of wine. Not that there were any places to order wine.

She was petite, dark-haired, dark-skinned, and very self-assured. Confidence was probably something required to brave the roadblocks and blown bridges with families in tow.

They continued twisting and turning their way south for another twenty minutes, then Kari Ann braked. Dylan and Akule both stood, looking over the cab of the truck. He shouldn't have been surprised, but he was.

An elderly man was sitting on one of those old bench wagons like Dylan had seen in an old western movie. The wagon was being pulled by a mare that had to be at least twenty years old. The guy was driving the wagon down the middle of the highway. He wore bib overalls and a worn baseball cap.

For some reason, that image poked at a memory in Dylan's mind. A decrepit truck passes an old man driving a horse and wagon.

Could have been a book he read.

Or maybe a scene from a movie?

Video game?

"Road into Dublin is blocked," the old guy warned.

Joshua leaned toward Kari Ann's window and said, "We're headed south. Trying to reach Brownwood."

"Not through Dublin, you're not. Road's blocked at Dublin. They're not letting anyone through. Me and Betsy had to turn around. Whole day wasted."

"Who is *they*?" Akule asked.

"Wouldn't know." The old man simply shrugged, as if the *who* of it didn't matter so much as the fact of it. He called "Let's go," to Betsy. She tossed her head and off they went.

Kari Ann pulled to the side of the road, walked around to the back of the pick-up, and dropped the tailgate. "Sorry, folks. I'm going to have to leave you here."

"But you're taking us to Santa Anna." Dylan slapped his Stetson against his leg. How could he get so dirty riding in the back of a truck? Too many caliche roads. His skin felt covered with the white powder that the truck's tires had stirred up.

"I'd hoped to," Kari Ann said. "I don't have time for the kind of detour you're going to have to make. Promised I'd get back to Glen Rose before dark so another one of Beverly's couriers could drive a group north—in this truck."

She unfolded a worn map and spread it across the lowered tailgate. "You're going to need to take this upcoming road west, through Rising Star. When you reach Cross Plains, head south. From there, southwest to Ballinger. I wish I could leave the map with you, but it's the only one I have."

Akule, Joshua, and Dylan all studied the map, committing it to memory as best they could.

"How far?" Dylan asked.

"I'm not sure." Kari Ann squinted at the map and used her thumb and forefinger to measure the lines. "A little more than a hundred miles from here to Ballinger. Another forty from Ballinger to San Angelo."

Joshua adjusted his pack and thanked her.

Akule looked as if she was ready to jog down the road.

Dylan wanted a horse.

Of course, that's why they were in this predicament to begin with. Because they wanted to retrieve their horses. *Their* horses. And the mule. He wasn't about to leave Fiona with that asshole Douglas Perkins.

Kari Ann gave them specific directions to find a guy named Blaine in Ballinger. "He can take you the rest of the way to San Angelo."

Blaine was the reason they'd had to split the group.

He was the one who would only take two people—three at the most. What difference did it make how many people they were taking? It wasn't like they were a party of twelve.

Kari Ann climbed back into the truck, which coughed to

life, sputtered then gained speed, disappearing in the direction they'd come.

Dylan hustled to catch up with Joshua and Akule. "A hundred miles. Crap."

"Cheer up, cowboy." Akule reached over and pushed his Stetson further down on his head. "If we can make twenty miles a day, we can be there in five days."

"Sounds like a goal to shoot for." Joshua looked up at the sky. "Good weather too, though I suspect it will change."

"Why do you say that?" Dylan asked. The sky was robin's egg blue. Not a cloud in sight.

"Knee hurts," Joshua said. "Pretty good barometer for a weather change."

"Explain to me how that works."

Dylan thought Akule was joking, giving Joshua a hard time. Joshua, however, took her question seriously.

"Barometric pressure. On average, the earth's atmosphere exerts a pressure per square inch of 14.7."

"You're kidding, right?" Dylan hadn't quite figured Joshua out yet. Hard to tell when he was being serious.

"I'm not kidding, Dylan. When the weather changes, the barometric pressure jumps up and down. If you've ever known anyone with migraines, they usually come down with a doozie right before a storm. Same principle."

"This guy's freaking amazing," Akule said in a mock whisper to Dylan.

"He definitely knows stuff."

"We should keep him around."

"How else would we know if the weather is about to change?"

Joshua smiled, almost as if he were enjoying the ribbing, and maybe he was. Maybe being here, walking down a dusty road that skirted around Dublin, Texas, was better than where he'd spent the last six months of his life.

If he thought this was good, he was going to love Alpine.

They made it to De Leon before sunset. Twelve miles. Four hours. And by the time they sought shelter in a half-burned-out Texaco station, the wind had shifted so that it was coming straight out of the north.

No clouds yet.

No rain or snow.

But Joshua was still favoring his left knee.

Dylan realized they were in a race. Not just against Perkins' thirty-day deadline. Not only because of their scant supplies. But because walking a hundred miles in a snowstorm didn't even remotely seem like something they could do.

CHAPTER 16

The horse trailer was dirty, and it smelled as if it had recently transported livestock.

"Don't want a clean trailer," Antoine had said when Keme commented on it. "I'm sorry. I know it's an unsanitary way to travel, but a clean trailer draws attention. That's something we can't afford to do."

"If smelling like horse shit will get us home faster, I don't mind one bit."

Antoine was stocky, mid-twenties, with jet-black hair and brown skin. "Beverly said you're experienced with a firearm."

"I am."

"You have it with you?"

Keme opened his jacket to reveal the Colt 45 in the shoulder holster. "Plus a backup Browning. Let's hope we don't need it."

"I hope we don't need either of them, but in case we do, I want you sitting at the back, near the door."

There was another door at the front of the trailer, one for people to hop in and check on the livestock. The double doors he was supposed to sit near were where ramps were positioned for loading and unloading animals. Along the length and at the back of the trailer were rectangular windows set at regular intervals, high enough that a horse could see out.

But they weren't transporting horses.

Twenty-one people, including Keme's family, huddled inside, sitting on haybales placed up against the trailer's walls. Once everyone was seated, there was a three-foot space in the middle running the entire length of the trailer. This is where everyone placed their packs.

"I want you here," Antoine was saying. "Watching our back. If you see anything, anything at all, you call me on this radio."

Keme accepted the handheld, surprised to be holding an electronic device that worked. But of course, shortwave radios didn't need GPS satellites. They simply needed to be charged. As long as someone had a way to do that, the radios would continue to work—until the batteries could no longer hold a charge.

"Since we're traveling at night, I don't expect any trouble."

"Will you run with the lights out?"

"I'd like to, but I don't want to hit a deer or javelina and flip the entire rig. I've disabled the tail lights. We'll keep the headlights on."

"Okay."

"Can you stay awake? I'm sorry to ask, but I need to know. We're putting these folks' lives in your hands and my hands."

"I'll stay awake."

"And you have no problem shooting, if it comes to that?"

Keme gestured toward his family. Paco sat with Pete on his left and Danny on his right, an arm wrapped around each. Claire held baby Lucy. "I'll have no problem if it comes to that."

Antoine nodded once, shook his hand, then said to Thomas, "Let's roll."

Thomas did not look nineteen. Thomas looked like he hadn't finished high school. He was skinny and had an awkward way about him like a teen who was still growing. Acne covered his cheeks, and Paco was certain he couldn't have grown a beard if his life depended on it. None of that mattered. What did matter was that he seemed comfortable with the Remington rifle he held.

Keme climbed into the trailer next to his family. Antoine slapped the doors shut, and they pulled out into the night.

There were sixteen other travelers, and as Bill had said, they varied in age from an old woman who had to be in her nineties to an infant younger even than Lucy.

This was precious cargo, and Keme was nearly overwhelmed by the responsibility of watching over them. He told himself that it was no different from riding patrol around Alpine, but seeing that newborn put what they were trying to do into a very clear perspective. They were, literally, saving lives.

The children fell asleep almost immediately.

The adults, even the ancient woman, kept their eyes open, gazes piercing through the window on the opposite wall as if they could see trouble coming. As if they could somehow prepare for it.

"How many of you are carrying a firearm?" Keme asked.

Two men and a young woman raised their hands.

"Are they loaded?"

All nodded in the affirmative.

"Be ready. Antoine doesn't expect any trouble, but if it comes it'll happen fast." He raised his voice to be heard over the noise of the road, which increased as they picked up speed. "Should we encounter trouble, I want everyone without a firearm to put the children in the middle of the trailer, on the floor, and cover them with your bodies."

Paco's eyes widened, and Claire pulled Lucy closer to her breast.

"Just a precaution. Better to think it through, talk it through, beforehand."

It was nine hours to the border. A total of five hundred and sixty-six miles if they took a direct route, which they would not. Adding in the detours and secondary roads, Keme thought they were looking at a twelve-to-fifteen-hour trip, at least. If everything went well, these folks could be to Candelaria before the following afternoon.

Keme and his family could be in Alpine by the time the sun rose. That thought woke him up, acting like a shot of caffeine to his system. Yeah, he could stay awake. He couldn't have slept if he tried, and he didn't plan on trying. He planned on standing guard over these people.

He'd heard Abuela say once that they each walked a path decided by the Creator even before they were born. "The Creator knows your path, Keme, even when you don't."

Keme didn't know if he believed that.

But this path—this part of their journey—was one that he felt uniquely qualified for. He wouldn't have been six months ago. But the days and weeks and months since June 6th had changed him in some fundamental way. Losing Lucy had awakened him to the fragility of life.

He didn't fear death, though he sometimes thought it would be better to die one way than another. Was it normal to dwell on such things? As Glen Rose fell behind them, as the old truck pulling the smelly horse trailer ate up the miles, Keme didn't focus on whether it would be better to die from the flu or a gunshot wound. Whether he'd rather die quickly or linger for a while. When had a person ever had any say in those things? Even when everything in this world worked, life was still unpredictable.

The creator knows your path, Keme, even when you don't.

Maybe so. His path, this day, was to protect these people—all of these people.

He would honor that.

He watched out the small windows. Walked from one side of the trailer to the other, though it was only a few feet. He wanted to stay loose. Didn't need his legs cramping when he needed them most.

They were well into the Texas hill country, near the town of Mason, when he first saw the taillights.

Keying the mic, he said, "Two vehicles, probably half a mile back."

"We see them," Thomas said.

"Can we outrun them?"

"We won't even try." It was Antoine's voice over the radio now. "Tell everyone it's about to get bumpy."

"Paco, wake everyone up. Tell them to hold on." Keme clipped the radio to his belt, pulled his pistol, and rested the barrel on the opening for the small window that faced the back of the trailer.

The truck slowed abruptly, causing a few people to bump into the person beside them. A boy about Danny's age slipped to the floor and woke crying. The truck fishtailed off the road, and it felt to Keme that they were driving across an unimproved pasture. Surely this wasn't a road.

Did Antoine know what he was doing?

"Everyone hold your position. Firearms ready in case we need them." Antoine's voice was calm and steady, as if he'd done this a dozen times. Maybe he had.

Keme saw that the three who'd said they had guns now had them out and were standing, looking out the side windows. The children had been placed in the middle, on top of the backpacks. Moms and dads and big sisters knelt beside them, whispering, assuring them that all would be okay.

Keme was still at the back doors, looking in the direction they had come. He slowed his breathing, looked down the site of his pistol. He saw first one, then another vehicle pass on the road they'd just left. They were traveling with their lights on. They were clipping along at what seemed like a dangerously high speed.

Highwaymen?

Other travelers?

Government personnel?

They waited a full ten minutes to be sure that the two vehicles didn't track back looking for them. Finally, Antoine's voice came over the radio. "Good job, everyone. I think we're in the clear, but we're going to take a more circuitous route, just to be safe."

So more than eight hours to Alpine.

Which was well worth it in Keme's opinion.

He'd rather get everyone there in one piece. If it meant going down unpaved county roads to do so, that was fine with him.

Their luck held most of the night. Through Junction and Sonora and Ozona. Always traveling a good distance from the main road. Staying off the interstate. Sticking to county roads, private roads, and twice crossing over pastures.

The wind began to blow from the north, but the stars still shone brightly overhead. He couldn't remember the last time he'd seen the light of a campfire or a vehicle or a home. It seemed as if it was just Antoine and Thomas and Keme and these families who simply wanted to find sanctuary. Who wanted to go home.

He began to hope, to believe they'd make it without being

assaulted. That they would slip through the night, unseen and unchallenged.

They turned toward Fort Stockton.

Nearly home.

Alpine only sixty-seven miles away.

He'd driven from one to the other a hundred times, maybe more. Never like this though. Never riding in a cattle trailer with family and strangers.

And then he was aware of something else.

His nostrils filled with the smell of it. His eyes began to burn. Adults woke and once again comforted their children. Paco joined him at the side window and let out a small gasp.

The fire seemed to stretch across the horizon. It seemed to sprout from the desert floor.

Through the faint early morning light, they were able to make out flames and smoke.

Fort Stockton was burning.

Akule was up before it was properly light.

The north wind caused the broken Texaco sign to slap against the building.

She was itching to go, and it irritated her that Joshua continued to snore and Dylan appeared dead. She tried prodding him with her foot to no avail. Who slept that soundly during the apocalypse?

Walking into the storage room, her eyes adjusted to the darkness and she saw empty shelves. Row after row of empty shelves. A two-wheel dolly had been abandoned near the loading bay doors, and a stack of pallets sat near the doors.

Pallets.

Wood.

Fifteen minutes later, she had a blazing fire going in the middle of what had been a Texaco convenience store. Once the water was boiling, she added tea leaves and pushed a mug into Dylan's and Joshua's hands. They thanked her, in a grunting sort of way, and did their best to appear awake.

"Twenty-six miles to Rising Star. Saw it scrawled on the counter by the empty register. We can make twenty-six miles in a single day, if we get going."

"Does she always wake up like this?" Joshua asked.

Dylan scrubbed a hand over his face. "Uh-huh."

"Hmm."

"Exactly."

"Eat your protein bars. We need to get going."

They ate, took care of their toiletry, and Joshua fastened two boards from the pallet together using duct tape. "Walking stick," he explained when she stared at him, impatiently tapping her foot.

The sun still wasn't properly up when they stepped out on the road, but pink and purple had begun to streak the eastern sky. Akule struggled against a rising uneasiness. She thought of the dream she'd had back home, in her apartment, before she'd told Tanda or her father that she was leaving. She couldn't remember if she'd had it again, but the images were poking her mind and her heart.

Terrible rains.

A river of blood.

A redbird.

An hour passed, then two. She focused on the road, on putting one foot in front of the other, on setting a fast pace. And then she stopped so abruptly that Dylan and Joshua shot past her.

"Ha. Knew you couldn't keep that pace up," Dylan teased.

She ignored him.

Standing in the middle of the road, she closed her eyes and listened intently. Then, she heard it again—something under the sound of the wind, beneath the desolation of this place. She slowly turned in a complete circle, scanning the horizon, listening.

A north wind.

Pasture fences.

Trees in the distance.

Dylan and Joshua had walked back toward her, watching but not interrupting. Waiting.

She held up a finger. There it was again. A dog's soft whine. But why would a dog be on a deserted road? Even dogs had the sense to get out of a cold wind.

She walked back in the direction they'd come from. Left the road on the north side. Stopped. Listened. When she heard the low whine again, she crossed back to the south side. The mutt was crouched down in the bar ditch, sitting in front of a rather large culvert that had been placed under the road. Which meant she'd walked directly over the dog and hadn't heard it.

Well, her conscious mind hadn't heard it.

But her heart had.

The dog was huge—maybe part St. Bernard, part Great Dane. Easily over a hundred pounds. Squatting, she held out a hand. "Here, boy."

"Seriously?" Dylan asked, but when she looked up he had a dopey smile on his face.

Joshua dropped his pack, began rummaging through it, and came up with a piece of jerky. He broke off the end and offered it to the dog.

"Now he's yours for life," Akule said.

"You're the one that stopped."

"I didn't feed him though." She adjusted her pack and once again set off down the road, still heading west.

The dog didn't follow, simply put his head down on his paws and whined. That was the sound she'd heard, and for reasons she couldn't explain, it resonated in her heart. Akule retraced her steps to him. "What is it, boy?"

Now his tail began to thump with reckless abandon.

When she reached for him, thinking she'd pet him on the head and earn his trust, he darted away and into the culvert where he began barking adamantly.

"Guess we should check it out." Dylan dropped his pack on the ground, got on his hands and knees, and climbed into the culvert. "Uh, guys. There's a man in here."

The dog bounded out, then sat with his tail thumping a fast rhythm on the ground. The man definitely belonged to the dog, or vice versa.

Akule crawled in after Dylan. They barely fit, but she was able to place her hand on the man's wrist. She checked his pulse, which was slow but steady. "Help me move him out into the light. Careful not to bump his leg."

Akule and Dylan had to basically drag him out by placing a hand under each armpit and pulling. They lay him in the grass. He was a large, burly man with reddish brown hair that reached to his shoulders and a long, unkempt beard.

"Leg's broke." Akule knew she was stating the obvious, but it wasn't every day a dog led you to a man in a culvert with a broken leg. What was he doing there? How did he get there?

"Better fix it now," Joshua said.

"The leg?"

"Yup."

"Okay."

Joshua held the man's shoulders while the dog whined and Dylan helped her to straighten the leg which had been grotesquely bent at an unnatural angle.

"I can't believe he didn't wake up for that."

"He probably passed out from the pain when he broke it, or maybe from shock after that." Akule glanced around. "Now we need a splint."

Joshua held up the walking stick he'd made from the boards of the packing crate. He handed it to her, and they used the oldest of their t-shirts, ripped into strips, to tie it to the man's leg.

When they'd done all they knew to do, when Akule was wondering if they could or should just leave him there, the dog walked over and began licking their patient on the face. The man stirred, assured the dog that he was fine, then finally realized he wasn't alone.

"Who are you?" he asked Akule.

"We were passing through. You looked like you could use a little help."

The man nodded as if that made sense. He stared down at his leg, and his face paled. "How'd I get here?" He seemed to suddenly realize his vulnerability. His shoulders tightened, and he blinked rapidly and reached for his dog.

"Good question." Joshua squatted beside him. He ran his fingers through his beard and spoke in a slow, measured voice. "We stopped because Akule heard your dog. He saved your life."

"Tiny's always been a good dog."

"Tiny?" Dylan assessed the dog. "Tiny?"

"He was small when he was a pup."

"Ah."

Joshua said he thought maybe the man owed Tiny his life, or at least the best dinner he could provide. "What's your name, son?"

"Buster. Buster Johnson."

Buster was thirty-two years old and had lived in the area all of his life. Two days earlier he'd been walking toward

Dublin for supplies when he'd nearly stepped on a rattle snake. "They usually aren't out this time of year. Guess the warm weather we had a few days ago brought him out. When I heard that rattle, I jumped a good three feet. Don't want to be bit by a rattler, let me tell you. Especially now that there's no 9-1-1."

"Did the snake bite you?" Akule made a move toward his pants leg, but Buster waved her away.

"Nope. Guess I scared him as much as he scared me. Problem was, when I jumped, I came down wrong, heard my leg snap." He stared at Tiny, running his hand through the dog's fur. "Guess I passed out after that."

"Your leg is broken," Akule confirmed. "But there are no bones sticking out. I think it'll heal okay."

"It's kinda coming back to me now. After it happened, and after that north wind started up, I realized I couldn't make it back home, so I crawled into the culvert. Been there—" He licked his lips and his eyes darted between the three of them then back to his dog. "A couple days, I'd guess."

"How far is it to your place?" Joshua asked.

"Mile and a half that way." He pointed north, across a pasture and toward some trees. "Back in that stand of live oaks. Can't see it from here, which I count to be a good thing."

Akule exchanged glances with Dylan and Joshua, but really there was nothing to discuss. They weren't going to leave Buster on the side of the road with only one good leg.

"Let's get you home," she said.

It was the wrong direction.

There was no way they'd make twenty-six miles now.

But it was the right thing to do.

They helped Buster to his feet. He slung one arm over Joshua's shoulders, the other over Dylan's. Akule walked behind the group of three, the massive dog Tiny by her side.

CHAPTER 17

Antoine pulled the truck to the side of the road when they crossed Highway 285 southeast of Fort Stockton. The sun had finally splashed rays of light across the desert, but to the north all they could see was a jagged line of flames through the smokey haze.

Antoine opened the side door.

Thomas opened the back doors.

Everyone piled out of the trailer and stood gawking at the scene of devastation in front of them.

"I wonder what started it."

"Was it set intentionally or was it an accident?"

"How long will it burn?"

Lots of questions. No one had answers. Keme, Paco, Antoine, and Thomas stepped away from the main group.

"What do we do?" Paco asked.

"What can we do?" Antoine shook his head. "It's probably best that we just keep going."

There was a clamor of hooves and they turned to see at

least twenty mule deer dart past. They were followed by a bobcat, slinking low to the ground.

If the animals were fleeing Stockton, Keme could only imagine what the people were doing.

"There might be people who need help," Claire said. She'd stepped away from the main group and now stood holding the baby and gazing to the north. Pete and Danny stood beside her, rubbing their eyes and yawning. "There might be families. . ."

The other passengers who had been riding in the trailer were taking advantage of the unexpected break to move to the side of the road and take care of their toiletry needs. A blanket from someone's pack was being held up for a measure of privacy. They all took a moment to stretch their legs, sip from water bottles, and watch the fire to the north.

Once they were all gathered again at the back of the trailer, Antoine put it up for a vote.

"We had planned to angle southwest on this dirt road, hit Highway 67, and take that into Alpine. There's another option though. We could continue west, which would parallel I-10. If there are any refugees from that fire, we might intercept them. I won't drive into Stockton. Won't take us closer, but I'll leave it to you all whether we dodge south or continue west."

The vote was unanimous.

Head west.

Keep an eye out for refugees.

After all, weren't they refugees?

Ten minutes later they came across the first family.

"Started in the middle of town." The old woman held the offered bottle of water to her grandchild's lips, cautioned her to drink in tiny sips, then took a small drink herself. "North wind caused it to spread quickly. No water to put it out. Nothing to do but run."

"Tried to leave two months ago, but the cabrón in charge

shot anyone who was caught on the other side of the fence. Fencing that had been put up around the center of town like it was a damn World War II camp." The man speaking was in his forties. Tears streamed down his face as he reached for his wife's hand. "Lived there all my life. Planned to raise our children there. I hate to see it burn, but that was no longer the town I grew up in."

"So how did you get away?" Paco asked.

"Gordo and his goons were fighting the fire, trying to save their precious supplies. People stampeded the fence and ran out into the desert. Scattered in every direction. If we hadn't come across you. . . "

"I guess we would have died," his wife finished.

By squeezing together, they managed to fit the family of six into the trailer.

The next group they picked up had to go in the back of the pick-up, which had very little open space owing to the fact that the horse trailer was a gooseneck.

Keme thought any other group would have to go on the roof of the trailer. Instead, they inched even closer and fit another family of four.

They were ten miles north of Alpine when Antoine stopped the truck. His voice cackled over the radio. "Perimeter guard. Looks like two men and a woman."

Which was all Keme needed to hear. He shot out of the back of the back doors. Ran to the front of the trailer, then the front of the truck. He heard Antoine telling him to get back, and he was aware of Paco hurrying to catch up with him.

Asking him who it was.

Asking him if it was safe.

He couldn't answer. Couldn't speak over the pounding of his own heartbeat. And then Tanda was off the horse and running toward them.

DYLAN HAD NEVER SEEN SO much crap shoved into one place.

Buster lived in a one-bedroom rock house that had to be a hundred years old. Every surface was crammed with stuff—most of it useless. Old newspapers. At least five televisions. Dishes and clothes and half-finished projects like a radio that had been taken apart but not put back together.

Cases and cases of dog food.

"Didn't know I'd have company, or I would've cleaned up," Buster joked.

There was a path of sorts through the piles. Tiny led the way. Dylan and Joshua helped Buster to the sofa, then stood looking around. There was nowhere to sit.

"I owe you people. I really do."

"Do you have anyone to help you out here, Buster?" Akule glanced around in concern.

"Nah. Me and Tiny, we're good on our own."

"Will you be able to. . ." Dylan nodded toward the busted-up leg.

"Yeah. Guess I'll have to."

That sat between them for a moment. Dylan wondered if the others were thinking what he was. That they couldn't take Buster with them. That they'd done the right thing, and now it was time to move on. He could practically feel Akule's impatience pulsing in the air, urging them to hit the road again.

"We probably need to get on then," Joshua said. "We wish you the best, Buster. Try to stay out of culverts."

"I wish there was a way I could thank you. After all, you didn't have to stop. Lots of people wouldn't."

Akule smiled and said, "Pay it forward, Buster."

"What's that mean?"

"Help the next person you meet who needs help."

"Yeah. Okay." They retraced the narrow path through the stacks, toward the back door, when Buster called out, "I don't suppose you all can use any vet supplies."

"Did he say vet supplies?" Dylan asked. His brain felt muddled, like he hadn't slept in days, like he wasn't truly awake. Why would a hoarder who lived alone with a large dog have a stash of vet supplies?

Joshua combed his fingers through his beard. "As in animals? Or veterans of the armed service?"

"Let's find out." Akule led the way back to the couch. "What kind of vet supplies, Buster?"

"I don't know. Don't have any animals except for Tiny. I looked through the boxes when everything first went dark. Didn't really see anything I could use other than the crates of dog food. Got real lucky there."

Akule moved a stack of magazines from the coffee table to the floor and perched on the edge of the table. "Where are these supplies, Buster?"

"Out back."

"Behind your house?"

"Right. I used to drive short-haul loads. After June 6th, didn't seem to be anyplace to take the stuff or anyone who could pay me for it, so—"

"The stuff's out back, behind your house?"

"Yup."

"And we have your permission to go through it?"

"It's not locked. Take whatever you want."

Fifteen minutes later they'd stuffed as much as they could possibly carry into their packs. Several times, Akule and Joshua consulted on what would be most important to take with them, on what would be most valuable. Finally, their packs were as full and heavy as they could reasonably manage.

Akule stood and hoisted her pack, staring around the

inside of the trailer in disbelief. "Pretty much explains the crates of dog food."

"This stuff would be good for trading if we had a way to transport it," Dylan said.

"But we don't." Joshua shook his head. "I wonder if Buster realizes what he has here. There have to be ranchers in the area who could use these supplies."

They went back inside to talk to Buster, but he was once again passed out. Tiny lay beside the couch, alert, ever the faithful companion. Dylan petted the dog's head while Akule glanced around. He felt as if he could read her thoughts at this point—they knew each other that well.

Traveling across an apocalyptic landscape did that to you.

You became known.

She couldn't bring herself to wake Buster. She understood that a broken leg was no small thing. Buster had been in tremendous pain as they'd moved him. She found a sharpie pen and wrote him a note on the back of a newspaper, then propped that up on the coffee table where he'd see it.

> *We took seven boxes of horse supplies. Thank you. Also, you should trade what's left in that trailer for food or ammo. There are bound to be ranchers nearby who need it.*

They were back on the road by noon headed toward Rising Star.

"Think what we have will be enough for Perkins?" Dylan asked.

"We'll offer him one box. The rest goes to Logan. Our horses in Alpine need it. As for Perkins, if one box isn't enough, deal's off and we'll find a way to take our horses."

"This guy sounds like a real piece of work." Joshua adjusted his pack. "I can hardly wait to meet him."

"The thing about Perkins is that when he starts talking he can be pretty persuasive. His decisions start sounding logical. It's insidious."

"Insidious?" Joshua ran his fingers through his beard as if he were trying to comb down a smile.

"Akule had a great SAT score," Dylan teased. "Especially the verbal section."

She bumped her shoulder into his, causing him to stumble and grin.

Joshua laughed at their antics, but his face grew serious as he studied the sky to the north. "Looks like my knee was right."

The clouds barreling toward them were dark, dense, and heavy with snow if Dylan wasn't mistaken.

"Looks like we better double-time it."

The storm caught up with them when they were still ten miles east of Rising Star.

Those last miles were like nothing Dylan had been through. The wind seemed intent on pushing them off course. The temperatures dropped so low that their breaths came out in plumes. Talking was impossible. They could barely see their way or each other or what might be lurking close by.

They stuck to the road.

Continued putting one foot in front of another.

And then when they were still three miles from town, Dylan grabbed Akule's arm and pointed to the south.

A house. Smoke from a chimney.

There was no way to know if whoever was there would be friend or foe. But walking in the storm was becoming impossible. She snagged Joshua's arm. They formed a circle.

Jerking her head toward the dim light in the distance, Akule shouted over the wind. "Do we take the risk?"

"Walking in this weather is a risk," Joshua pointed out.

Dylan shifted from foot to foot. "Let me approach first. You two wait—"

But Akule was already detouring toward the house.

Joshua slapped him on the shoulder, shouted to be heard over the wind. "It's a good thing—a woman who knows her mind."

Dylan would normally have agreed, except when they were trudging through a storm toward a house that might be filled with homicidal survivalists.

The last thing they wanted to do was sneak up on an encampment and get shot.

He and Joshua jogged to catch up with Akule.

She was stepping onto the front porch by the time they reached her side. She raised her hand to knock on the door when it was thrown open. A giant man stood there, rifle in hand. His salt-and-pepper beard was trimmed like a goatee. Conversely the top of his head was bald. He leaned forward, peered past them, then said, "Get in, quick. You're letting out all the heat."

CHAPTER 18

Tanda threw herself into Keme's arms. He held her close, wrapped his arms around her so tightly that he could believe what was happening was real.

Not an illusion.

Not a dream.

Real.

His family was safe. He'd made it home. This postmodern world wasn't something he would ever wish on his worst enemy. There was danger, deprivation, and heartache waiting around every corner. Being in Alpine wouldn't fix all of those things.

It wouldn't make their lives safe and whole again.

But it would make them bearable.

"Thank God," she said over and again. Finally, she pulled away, looked at him, and smiled.

She didn't ask where the horses were. Didn't ask why he was riding in the back of a horse trailer. He could practically watch her process what was happening, adjust her course, and he wasn't a bit surprised that she immediately took charge.

"Liam, lead this truck into town. Put everyone in the Sul Ross Student Center. While you're there, send someone to alert Dixie and have her activate our emergency volunteers. We need to feed these people and give them a place to rest."

Miles had also dismounted and joined them. He slapped Keme on the back, welcomed him home, then asked, "Does anyone need immediate medical attention?"

"I think basically they're all okay, but you'll want to do a more thorough assessment once we're in town." Keme waved toward the horse trailer. "Half these people, we picked up on the road just north of here. Stockton is burning."

"We're aware. We have extra patrols out, looking for folks." Tanda glanced to the north, toward the storm clouds that were building and the smoke that was staining the horizon.

"Put me with a patrol," Keme said. "I want to help."

"Go with your family, Keme. Take them into town." She'd walked with him to the back of the trailer. Taking a quick look inside, she seemed to finally register that Akule and Dylan weren't with him. "Where are they?"

"A few days behind us. Hopefully. I'll explain later."

"Okay." And then she was in the trailer, hugging Paco, speaking softly to Claire, brushing a hand over Danny's hair, Pete's arm, and little Lucy's cheek. "Welcome home. We have prayed for you, thought of you, every single day."

She backed out of the trailer and spoke to the entire group of refugees. "Welcome to Alpine. We don't have a lot, but what we have we'll share. You'll receive medical aid, food, and a place to rest at the university."

The grandmother asked, "How much farther?"

"Twenty minutes."

The grandmother nodded, then ducked her head and spoke to a child in Spanish.

Keme climbed back into the trailer. Tanda slapped the

doors shut, and he heard her giving directions to Antoine. Keme glanced up, looked out the horse windows, and saw Miles as he reclaimed his horse's lead. Liam trotted his horse past them and shouted to Antoine, "Follow me." Tanda turned to speak to Miles. He heard the words *Akule, Dylan, a few days behind.*

As they picked up speed he saw the Alpine city limit sign, Big Bend Saddlery, the Feed and Supply, and the Maverick Inn.

Years later, he would look back on those few minutes as some of the most poignant of his life. Trying to beat the storm. Recognizing the exhaustion that seemed to permeate his bones. The stench of fire in the air. A low-level nausea caused by concern for the children. Worry that the trip had been too much. And beneath all of that relief—so much relief—that Paco and Claire, Pete and Danny and Lucy were home, within the sanctuary of Alpine. An aching awareness that Akule and Dylan and Joshua weren't.

It all coalesced into a painfully clear focus that spoke to the precious nature of life and family and community.

They made a right onto the Sul Ross campus.

Antoine dropped the truck into a lower gear so that he could follow Liam who was on horseback. The truck lumbered up the road to the university on the hill that looked out over Alpine.

Keme became aware that the people crowded into the trailer had turned their gaze to him. Paco and Claire shot him a questioning look. Pete and Danny glanced from their grandfather to their parents. And Keme tried to smile. He tried to find the words to assure them that finally, they were safe, or as safe as one could be.

But no words came.

The tears slipping down his cheeks might have concerned

them, or the fact that he sat on one of the hay bales, dropped his head in his hands and wept.

For the first time in his life, Keme truly understood what it meant to come home.

For Akule, the next forty-eight hours passed like scenes from a dream she couldn't quite remember. A caravan of travelers had taken shelter in the home. They sat around the living room, lined the walls really, scooting closer together and making room for her and Dylan and Joshua.

The fire succeeded in heating the room, or maybe it was the press of bodies. The wind continued to howl outside. Ice began to hit the windows with sharp, continuous pings. The rain and sleet against the roof—which must have been metal—was a virtual cacophony of sound.

Cacophony. A combination of discordant sounds.

She'd studied that one for the SAT test, which she had scored well on. She'd even been offered a couple of scholarships to attend Sul Ross and Tarleton and Texas State—small schools but with a solid reputation. She hadn't accepted though. Instead she'd immersed herself in what she came to think of as her lost years. She bounced between Houston and Austin. She depended on friends, and when she'd worn out her welcome there, she'd become homeless. Insisting to herself that she loved the freedom, that she didn't need anyone, that she was okay alone.

She was not okay alone.

It was a call home that had turned everything around. She'd borrowed a woman's cell phone. The woman was a social worker who checked on the *bridge people* at least once a week. Her hands shaking, Akule had punched in her parents' number. Her mother had answered, told her to come home, told her that everything would be okay.

She hadn't judged her, lectured her, or screamed that Akule had broken her heart several times over. She'd simply said, "Come home." And Akule had.

She thought of that younger self, weak and exhausted and lost. How was it that she felt stronger now, even in the midst of this dysfunctional world? Why was it that she no longer felt lonely? She sat huddled in a room of strangers, a very long way from home, a winter storm surging outside. They had little food, few supplies, and no real plan.

Joshua caught her gaze and offered a thumbs up.

She glanced at Dylan and smiled. He reached for her hand and interlaced his fingers with hers.

Instead of pulling away, Akule closed her eyes, rested her head against the wall, and allowed the burdens she'd been carrying slip off for a moment.

She must have slept, because she woke to people shuffling about, donning backpacks, and traipsing into the kitchen for a cup of water or to the back of the house to use the facilities. The sky outside wasn't exactly light, but it would be soon. The sleet and ice had mercifully stopped.

Dylan and Joshua stood before the man who had answered the door.

Akule joined them. "Tell me you planned to wake me up."

"We wouldn't have left you," Dylan said, nudging her shoulder with his, then offering her a piece of jerky. She took it, pulled off a small bite, and wondered at the fact that it actually tasted good.

"I might be able to fix it," Joshua was saying. "Mind if I take a look?"

"Not my vehicle, man. I ride a four-wheeler with an electric battery that I recharge with solar panels. Takes forever to recharge, but it works."

"Where is Cheyenne's car?"

"We pushed it under the carport. If you want to take a look at it, she wouldn't mind."

"What's going on?" Akule asked.

Joshua was already walking out, walking toward Cheyenne's car and the carport, asking what tools their host had available.

"Big guy with a goatee is Waylon Jennings."

"Like the singer?"

"Exactly. No relation. The people here are all packing up. I guess they have horses and took shelter in this house when the storm hit."

"But Cheyenne has a car."

"Yup. One that doesn't run." He nodded toward a woman who looked to be in her 50s. Her hair was cut short in a haphazard way. She was going through her pack, tossing things that she obviously was ditching into a pile.

Akule walked over to her. "Cheyenne?"

"Yup." The woman didn't look up.

"I'm Akule. This is Dylan."

Cheyenne continued discarding items.

"What are you doing?" Dylan asked.

"Deciding what I can carry, and what I can't. What does it look like I'm doing?"

"Our friend, Joshua, is taking a look at your car."

"Yeah, well, I wish him luck. That piece of shit machine has breathed its last if you ask me."

"Joshua's pretty good with stuff. If he can get it going—"

Finally, Cheyenne's hands stilled, and she looked up at them. It seemed to Akule that her eyes held a world of misery and disappointment tinged with a good dose of exhaustion. “He won’t.”

“Where are you headed?”

“What does it matter to you?”

“It’s a simple question.”

“Bethel. I’m headed to Bethel.” She zipped her pack shut and stared forlornly at the pile of discarded items.

“We need to get to Ballinger. If Joshua gets your car running, will you give us a ride?”

“He won’t,” but her voice was a tad less certain this time. Hope had crept in. “What was he. . . a mechanic before June 6th? Because he didn’t look like a mechanic.”

“Nah. He’s just a guy who knows stuff.” Dylan held out a hand, as did Akule. Together they pulled Cheyenne to her feet.

“Right. Okay. Yes, I’ll give you a ride—if he has it fixed by sunrise. Because one way or another, I’m leaving as soon as the sun splits that horizon.”

With that she stormed off to the back of the house.

“All personality, that one,” Dylan said.

“Do you really think that Joshua can fix her car?”

“I don’t know, Akule. He is a guy who knows stuff.”

Forty minutes later, they were crammed into her small Volkswagen Beetle. With everyone’s packs—Cheyenne’s now repacked with the stuff she wouldn’t be leaving—it was a tight fit, but no one complained. Cheyenne drove. Joshua rode up front so he could keep his eye on the check engine gauge. Akule and Dylan were crammed into the back seat with the bags.

The roads were deserted.

They didn’t pass a single car, horse, or person walking.

And they made it to Ballinger in record time.

Amazing how fast traveling was when you weren’t walking.

Cheyenne let them out on the outskirts of town. She took

off as soon as they'd shut the door, spewing gravel and causing Dylan to jump back.

Now all they had to do was find Blaine.

Akule didn't mind walking again, though the day was cold and the wind still from the north—not a gale like the day before, but enough to make her burrow her hands in her pockets and tuck her chin down.

They followed Beverly's directions, and they found Blaine's place exactly where it was supposed to be. An RV tucked into some trees on a few acres. A large pile of firewood had been chopped and stacked a few feet from the trailer. Panels of plyboard painted with camouflage encircled the immediate vicinity around the RV. If they hadn't known what to look for, they would have walked right by it.

Now they stood there, staring and trying to wrap their minds around what they were seeing. Akule, Joshua, and Dylan all understood immediately why Blaine would take only two persons, never more than three. Akule took one look at the contraption he expected them to climb into and turned to look out across the fields.

Would walking be so bad?

It was only another forty-one miles.

As if he could read her thoughts, Dylan said, "It still hasn't climbed above freezing, and the wind is blowing from the north."

"The sleet stopped."

"For now it has. But it could start up again any minute."

"So what are you saying? That we should get in that thing?"

"Yeah. That's exactly what I'm saying."

The small prop airplane looked to be vintage World War II. An older man working on the engine looked up, then wiped his hands on a greasy rag. He walked over to them. "Can I help you folks?"

Akule couldn't think of a single word to say.

Was she going to get into that rusty bucket?

"Joshua Andrews. These are my friends—Dylan and Akule. Beverly Skinner sent us here. Said you could take us to San Angelo."

"Sure. I can do that. Since Beverly sent you, I'd be happy to do so. That woman is a saint."

Akule managed to ask, "Are you sure that thing is. . . is safe?"

"Akule has a fear of heights," Dylan offered. "She's thinking about walking in this weather, if you can believe that."

"I do not have a fear of heights. I have a fear of dying, and I can speak for myself, thank you."

Dylan held up both hands, palms out. Joshua and Blaine exchanged a knowing look that made Akule want to stamp her foot.

"My plane is a 1939 Bücker Jungmann BU-131," Blaine said. He was an old man, skin thin as tissue paper, age spots peppering his hands and neck. He spoke with a heavy European accent. "I can get you there, and I don't advise walking like the girl suggested because the gangs in San Angelo have been on the prowl, if you know what I mean."

Blaine didn't waste any time. Opening the trailer, he shouted to Patches that he'd be back and not to eat the furniture. Akule's heart rate notched up and her palms began to sweat.

There were seats for the pilot plus one more. Akule could cram into the second seat with Joshua. A third person would have to sit on the floor in the back. "Looks like I'm riding cargo," Dylan said, climbing into the back before she could argue with him.

Not that she planned to argue with him.

At least her seat had a seatbelt.

Before she could think of a really solid reason not to do this, one that even Dylan would agree with, Blaine was in the pilot seat, flipping switches and murmuring sweet nothings to his vintage aircraft. Joshua stood in front of the plane. When Blaine gave him the signal, he pulled down on the propeller.

The engine roared to life.

Blaine hollered, "Get in," and Joshua scrambled onto the wing, then squeezed into the seat with Akule.

She didn't need to worry about the seatbelt. She was packed in tighter than mackerel in a barrel. Blaine could turn his little plane upside down and she wouldn't fall out.

She prayed he wouldn't turn the plane upside down.

The plane shook. The noise was tremendous and the air was absolutely frigid. Akule had the bizarre mental image of flying inside a refrigerator.

The landing, on a remote airstrip outside the state park, was even more terrifying than the take-off. She couldn't get out of the back seat fast enough. Joshua shook Blaine's hands, making a suggestion for how he might improve the plane's rocky ride. Akule resisted the urge to kiss the frozen ground. As for Dylan, he crawled out of the back pulling his pack behind him and pushing his trusty Stetson onto his head.

Thirty minutes later they were walking down Perkins' dirt lane, passing the piece of plyboard with the large red letters which still read—

Stop and turn back
Trespassers will be shot

"Watch your head, Dylan." Akule tried to pass it off as a

joke. In truth, this place was already giving her the creeps and they were barely on the property.

"Very funny." He pushed his Stetson more firmly down on his head, as if it could protect him, and grinned at her.

"I trust you'll explain the joke to me one day."

"Yes, Joshua. We absolutely will."

But her stomach again felt nauseous, as if this were the critical point in their journey. It wasn't. They'd made it to the metroplex and back. This shouldn't be that hard.

Somehow though, she suspected it would be.

The walking path was still uncomfortably narrow, crowded with old farm equipment to the right and left. They'd continued for another five minutes when an all-too-familiar person appeared around a curve in the lane, still riding a horse, still sporting a cocky smile.

"You two again."

"Yeah, it's us again. Before you move to bash me in the head, we're here because your boss wants to see us."

Akule's hand was on her hip holster. "Bash him in the head again, and I'll shoot you."

"Chill." He jerked a chin toward Joshua. "What about him?"

"He's with us. So just lead the way, okay?"

And surprisingly, he did.

CHAPTER 19

They walked to the main house and were ushered onto the same back porch where the same old lady was sitting in the corner and a fire once again burned in the chiminea. She didn't seem surprised to see them, didn't look up at all from her bird-watching.

Dylan stared at the couch. He couldn't resist the urge to press his fingertips to the back of his head.

"Everything's good back there," Akule teased, but her voice was tight.

Joshua walked over to the chiminea, pulled off his gloves, and held his hands out to the fire. "This place is just as you two described it."

They heard Douglas Perkins before they saw him. Boots across the Italian tile. He appeared in the doorway between the back porch and the living room, filling the space with his bulk and condescending attitude.

"Back sooner than I expected."

"We're here for the animals," Akule said. She'd already

pulled one of the boxes of equine supplies out of her pack. Now she set it on the table in front of the couch. "Zinc oxide cream, Betadine, dewormer, and ophthalmic ointment—basically a first aid kit for horses."

Dylan thought Perkins must have been a great poker player in his previous life. He didn't look surprised in the least. Didn't step toward the precious supplies. Instead, he stuck his hands in his pockets and pinned his attention on Akule. "That's it?"

"Yes, that's it. Now, where did you put our animals?"

But Perkins was shaking his head.

Dylan had a nearly irresistible urge to slug the guy.

"Not so fast. An equine first aid kit for three horses and a mule? Do you realize what I can sell those animals for?"

"Those aren't your animals to sell."

Perkins shrugged. "You know what they say about possession being nine-tenths of the law."

Dylan drew his gun without fully realizing what he was doing. "I know what they say about the Castle Law."

"You're standing in my house, son. The Castle Law would only apply to me." But Perkins looked worried. He hadn't expected Dylan to draw down on him.

"Your house. Our animals. And I see you have a pistol in that holster on your hip, which meets the requirement for aggravated robbery. Where are the horses?"

"And the mule," Akule added.

"And the mule."

It was Joshua who walked into the middle of the stalemate—literally. He stepped between Dylan and Perkins.

"Let's try to keep this civil."

"Who are you?"

"He's our friend," Akule said.

"He's family," Dylan clarified.

Perkins sighed heavily as if they were interrupting his busy schedule, walked over to the old woman in the corner, bent down, and said something to her. Then he escorted her out of the room. For a fraction of a second, Dylan saw an expression of compassion flit cross Perkins' face. So, there was a human heart beating somewhere inside the man.

When Perkins returned, he walked over to the table, picked up the kit, and stared at it. Finally, he shook his head. "I don't know where you got this, but it's not enough."

"We had a deal," Akule reminded him.

"Yes. Our deal was that if you returned in thirty days—"

"Which we did." Dylan really wanted to punch Perkins in the face, erase the smirk if only for a moment.

"And if you brought something of value to cover the cost of the animals' feed, then I would return them."

Akule dropped her pack, unzipped it, and pulled out the whiskey and honey. "Your wife wanted these for her medical supplies. We're also giving you equine supplies that you can't find anywhere else. I'd say that's a fair trade."

"How long do you think this single box of supplies will last?"

"That's not my problem."

"But our trade parameters are your problem, and I'm telling you this does not cover what I spent feeding three horses and a mule."

Joshua once again raised a hand, held it out, and pressed it down three times as if to pat the aggression out of the air. "What would be fair?"

"I don't know. But this isn't."

"A bit ambiguous."

Perkins stared at Joshua and maybe for the first time he saw more than an old man with a gray beard. Maybe, Dylan thought, he saw a man who knew things. A man who might be able to solve a problem.

Joshua jerked his head toward the window. "I noticed three guys standing around your pump house."

"And?"

"And I suspect that means your pump is broken."

Perkins didn't speak. He waited, his attention now pinned completely on Joshua.

"I'll fix the pump, and you'll return the animals and the saddles Akule and Dylan left here. You return every single piece of equipment that was tethered on those horses. And we'll need to see the animals first, to confirm you've given them adequate care."

"You think you can fix my pump?"

"If I can't, no harm no foul. We'll be on our way and you can keep the animals."

"Joshua—"

Joshua silenced Akule with one shake of his head.

"Deal." Perkins held out his hand. Joshua grasped the man's hand, and as he did, he said, "Be true to your word, Mr. Perkins. Otherwise, we will take what is ours, by force."

Ten minutes later they dropped their packs in the pre-fab home—the same small dwelling they'd been in before. Their saddles and pads were still stacked against one wall.

Akule walked to her saddle and ran her fingers across the leather. Dylan wondered if she would say what they were both thinking or push her concerns back down. He didn't have to wonder for long.

"What if you can't fix it?"

"I should be able to."

"Should?"

Joshua spoke calmly, reasonably. "He wasn't going for it,

Akule. We would have had to take the animals by force. At least this way, there's a chance that he will keep his word. And I'm sure these people need water. I don't mind spending a few hours fixing their pump."

It took more than a few hours.

That afternoon, the next day, and the day after that, Akule and Dylan cared for the animals, visited with Franklin who wanted to know more about Alpine, and paced the small living area.

"Joshua will get it working," Dylan assured her, and he hoped he was right. He didn't see Akule leaving the animals. He certainly wasn't looking forward to a shoot-out. They were vastly outnumbered. Fighting Perkins was one thing. Fighting his entire group of survivalist friends was another thing entirely.

But it wasn't necessary.

Joshua fixed the pump.

Perkins begrudgingly said they were free to go.

Three days later, they were saddled up and riding away from San Angelo. The weather had turned again, sleet spitting down on them, temperatures miserable.

They could have looked for a place to hunker down, but by that time they could practically smell Alpine around the corner. It was a unanimous decision.

Brave the weather.

Push through to Alpine.

It was a decision they would question for the rest of their lives.

THREE HUNDRED MILES.

They pushed the horses as much as they dared. Rode

through the weather. Slept as little as possible. Stopped for only a few hours each night. Crossed I-10 at Sheffield. There was no need to skirt Dryden, or so a teenager they'd passed on the road had claimed. The teen was correct. A large part of Dryden had burned since they'd been through. The small town appeared to be completely deserted.

Two-thirds of the ride was behind them.

Sanderson was twenty miles away. They'd stop there. Sleep properly. Check on Stella and Jimbo, Lester and Dorothy.

The weather deteriorated even more. The temperature plummeted and the rain turned to sleet. What little light there had been began to fade.

Six miles west of Dryden, as they were passing what had been the regional airport, they were surprised by a young woman standing in the middle of the road, waving her arms.

"Stop. Please stop."

Akule reigned in her mare. Dylan and Joshua did the same.

The woman was slight, with stringy hair, ragged jeans, and mismatched tennis shoes. The coat she wore hung on her slight frame like clothes on a scarecrow. She ran toward them. Akule instinctively backed up and put her hand to her weapon.

Dylan did the same.

Joshua hollered, "Don't come any closer, ma'am."

When she stopped, he added, "What's the problem?"

"My boyfriend. He was thrown off his horse."

"Your horse?" Akule looked left and right. Darkness had nearly fallen, and she saw no sign of a horse or a boyfriend. A memory pricked her mind.

Rain falling.

A trail of blood.

A redbird.

"He's there, behind that station. We managed to walk over

there, but he's hurt real bad. Can't you. . . can't you just look at him and see if you can help?"

Akule looked to Dylan, who nodded once, as did Joshua.

But Joshua walked his mare closer, lowered his voice. "Stay in the saddle though. In case it's a trap."

It was the right thing to do—maybe. They were all thinking of Buster and his giant dog Tiny. But this woman wasn't Buster, and there was no dog, no animal to indicate whether coming closer would be wise or foolish.

"We can't stay," Akule said. "But we'll see if we can help."

They'd barely turned the corner behind the station when two men attacked. The first pulled a knife and without hesitating, without a warning of any kind, reached up and plunged it into Dylan's side, then yanked down on the handle.

It flashed through Akule's thoughts that the pain must have been incomprehensible. Her mind reeled to grasp what was happening even as blood poured from Dylan's wound. There wasn't enough light to see well, the sleet had increased, and the horses were frightened. She worked to calm Daisy. They couldn't lose the horses. They'd die out here without the horses.

Time slowed like the cell phone videos she once took. . . events occurring in slow motion with startling detail.

Fiona brayed loudly and yanked hard on the lead rope.

Dylan managed to stay in the saddle. He swung Texas Lady's head left, knocked the man off his feet, pulled his gun and shot him.

Joshua's horse reared at the blast of gunfire. Joshua landed on his backside, popped up, and fought his assailant.

Akule dismounted to help Joshua back onto his horse. She pulled her gun, but she couldn't decide who to shoot. Too many targets. And what if she hit one of the animals or one of her own group by mistake?

The girl who had laid the trap charged toward her, arm pulled back, hand clenched in a fist. Akule sidestepped and bumped into Daisy who whinnied and attempted to dance away. The woman's fist slammed into Akule's eye, causing her head to jerk back and her vision to fill with flashes of white light.

She heard Dylan whistle for the horses.

Akule shook her head, saw Dylan attempting to grab their leads without dismounting. His entire side was slick with blood. She was standing close enough to smell it, to see it saturating his jeans.

They might have won at that point if the two men and the girl had been all there was to fight.

But a third man rode out of the storm, urged his mount into a gallop, and charged directly at Joshua. The horse collided with Joshua, and he sank to the ground like a punctured balloon.

The man turned to charge Akule.

Dylan fired twice.

Akule realized he'd hit the man when his left arm jerked back. Instead of stopping, instead of standing his ground, the man turned and galloped off into the darkness.

Akule took aim in his direction.

Fired. Heard someone cry out.

Dylan used his good leg to urge Texas Lady forward. He made it next to Joshua. "Grab my stirrup. Pull yourself up."

"I can't..." was all the old guy managed.

And then Akule was at Joshua's side, calming Amber and pushing Joshua up into the saddle, grabbing Fiona's lead, vaulting up onto her horse.

They heard the sound of hoofbeats, and Akule figured asshole number three was heading back for more. But she'd shot him. Dylan had shot him. How was the man still riding?

Maybe it was someone else.

How many were there in this group?

Her terror and confusion gave way to anger. She was all for fighting until the last assailant was dead. But her vision had tunneled to a small speck.

She heard Dylan say, "Grab Fiona's lead, Joshua. Let's go. Now!"

They galloped off into the darkness, traveling south of the road, plunging into the sleet and snow and wind. They rode hard. Direction didn't matter. Surviving mattered. Akule had no concept of how much time had passed, of how much space they'd put between their group and the goons behind them.

Twice she stopped.

Spoke to Joshua in a low whisper.

He simply shook his head. "Later. Let's put more distance between us."

Then she went to Dylan's side, checked the knife wound, told him that he couldn't die on them now. "Not here. Not like this."

The expression on his face, which she could barely see by the beam of her flashlight, was a mosaic of concern. She wanted to wipe his worries away. Wanted to kiss him and assure him that all was well. Why hadn't she kissed him? What would she do if she lost him?

"Can you stay in the saddle, Dylan?"

He didn't seem able to speak. Possibly he couldn't find the words. She suspected he was in shock now from the blood loss and the pain. His head sank forward. His entire body dipped towards the saddle.

She pressed a t-shirt against his side, and the jolt of pain brought him back into full consciousness.

"Sorry," she whispered. Then she was back in her saddle, and they were moving again.

She wondered if they were headed in the right direction.

She wondered if it even mattered anymore.

And then she stopped wondering. Her mind went numb. She had nothing to move forward on—no energy, no bright ideas. Only instinct. It would have to be enough.

CHAPTER 20

They rode through the night. Stopped to apply fresh bandages to Dylan and Joshua. Rode through the day and into the next night. Marathon was too far. But they couldn't stop. There was nowhere to stop. They were in a virtual no-man's land now. The horses slowed to a walk. Then slower still. Barely an amble. Akule understood the animals were as exhausted as they were.

Hungry.

Cold.

Homesick.

Fine slivers of sleet continued to pellet them. The weather swirling around them had taken on the quality of a malevolent snow globe. What would come at them next? How would they see it in time to react? How could they possibly defend themselves?

Dylan and Joshua rode side by side. Akule followed behind them, leading Fiona and watching carefully should one or the other fall out of their saddle. How had these two men come to mean so much to her? How had they found a way past her well-placed walls?

But they had.

Joshua, whom she'd known such a short time, reminded her of *Abuela*—quiet, wise, direct. He was *one of the good ones*, as the old folks were fond of saying. Akule thought she understood that phrase now. How would they have found Paco and his family within the masses of the tent city? Joshua had taken a risk. For them. For people he didn't even know. She also realized that if it hadn't been for him, their animals would still be with Douglas Perkins.

How long would it have taken to walk home?

How would they have fled vagabonds and killers on foot?

They had needed Joshua, though they hadn't realized it.

As for Dylan, Akule couldn't describe what she felt for him. Her emotions changed, dipped, soared—constantly becoming more complicated. Attempting to label those feelings only made her head and her heart ache.

She hadn't wanted him to come.

Had wanted to insist that he go away when he'd stopped her on the street in Alpine. She'd thought he was a thrill seeker, and that he would only slow them down.

Now she understood that almost from the start he'd become an essential part of their team. Had she really thought she and her father could do it alone? What had she been thinking? How could she have been so prideful? Dylan—he was the other half she hadn't known she'd been missing.

The blow he'd taken to the skull had landed them inside the Douglas home. Otherwise, they'd simply have been escorted off the property. Or shot. They wouldn't have ridden in the horse trailer to Dallas. They might not have arrived in time to find her brother. Dylan didn't complain. He worked hard. And that cocky smile appeared just when she needed to see it.

She knew he was her friend.

Was what she felt for him more? Was that even possible in their world? Immediately images of Cade and Harper, Stella and Jimbo, Paco and Claire popped into her mind. But their love for one another had existed before June 6th.

Was anyone falling in love now?

It seemed like such a frivolous thing.

Or a necessary one.

What she knew with absolute certainty was that she owed a great debt to him. If it hadn't been for Dylan, she'd most likely be dead—killed by a drifter's knife. Even as she had that thought, Dylan pressed a hand to his side, applying pressure to the knife wound.

"Is it bleeding again?" Akule had to practically shout to be heard over the wind and ice and general misery.

He shook his head, then attempted to smile back at her, but it came across more like a grimace.

Joshua's foot was leaving a line of blood.

A trail of blood. Rain. A redbird.

They'd need to rewrap his foot soon. At least no one could follow that red trail, not in this weather. Though honestly, their direction wouldn't have been difficult to figure out. Where else could they have gone? Marathon was the only possible stop this side of Alpine.

Akule's right eye had swollen shut completely. The world in front of her looked frozen, uninviting, and slightly skewed. If her eighteen-year-old self could see her now, could see them, would anything be different? Would she have made different choices, before the world changed? What about a month ago, before they'd left Alpine?

Would she have gone forth so boldly?

And yet, they had been successful.

Paco, Claire, and their three children were safely in Alpine. She had to believe they were. She couldn't bear the thought that they, too, might have been attacked or injured and still traveling in this weather. No. They were home. It was both a hope and a prayer.

Let them be home.

As they plodded through the miserable weather, she tried to focus on what they'd accomplished. The horses were tired and hungry and needed water, but they'd reclaimed them from Douglas Perkins. They were bruised and bleeding, but they weren't beaten. Marathon lay ahead.

They would stop at the Gage.

They didn't really have a choice.

There were no fresh tracks that she could see, but then she was peering down with one eye. Maybe they were alone. Maybe the world had forgotten this place.

Highway 90 merged with Highway 385 as they crossed into Marathon. Through the swirling ice and snow she could make out a gas station, the Big Bend Information Center, a gift shop. The horses picked up speed, somehow aware that they were at last near shelter. Possibly they instinctively understood that each step brought them closer to home.

Or she could have been imagining those things.

Certain that no one was behind them, she urged Daisy forward and trotted to the front of the group. "Let me be sure..." was all she managed to say. Though it was early afternoon, darkness was falling.

There were no lights.

No indication of fires.

Surely, if anyone were left alive in this town, they would be huddled around a fire. They would be in one of the buildings, sheltering, seeking sanctuary.

She led the ragtag group to the Gage Hotel. The animals definitely remembered the place. Daisy pushed forward into the shelter of the courtyard.

"I'll take care of the horses," Dylan mumbled, but he couldn't even get out of the saddle by himself.

Joshua practically fell off his horse, stumbling when his injured foot attempted to hold the weight of his body. Somehow he still helped her to lower Dylan from his saddle. They nearly dropped him on the ground, then the three staggered into the main lobby.

Everything was as they'd left it.

The couches and chairs pulled into a small circle.

The ashes from their breakfast fire still in the hearth.

She stared at the pillows they'd gathered from a few of the rooms, thought of resting her head on one, and nearly gave in to the temptation. The sound of ice hitting the window panes pulled her out of her reverie.

"Stay here. I'll see to the horses and then get firewood."

"I'll help." Joshua tried to stand, again stumbled when he put his weight on his left foot, and fell back onto the couch.

"Go through our supplies. See what you can find for us to eat."

They all knew there was very little food left, but Joshua nodded and dropped his pack to the floor.

It had rained since they'd been at the hotel last, but the water in the courtyard's fountain had frozen over. They'd carried buckets of water from the trough outside the pump house when they'd been at the hotel before. She knew that water would be frozen as well. Might as well stay in the courtyard where she was at least protected from the worst of the wind. Akule found a shovel in the gardening shed, busted up the ice in the fountain, filled a bucket with it, and took it inside.

Joshua had somehow started a blaze in the fireplace. They were past caring if anyone saw them. It seemed impossible. It seemed that in this corner of the world, they were on their own.

"Help me move him closer," Akule said.

It ended up being easier to move the couch with Dylan on it. He'd passed out. Sweat beaded his forehead, and he shivered though Joshua had tucked a sleeping bag around him.

Akule remembered something she'd seen the last time they were here, walked down the hall into one of the luxury suites, and retrieved the large iron pot filled with silk flowers. Dumping the flowers on the floor, she carried the pot outside, filled it with ice, and brought it in to set on the fire next to the bucket.

She sat there, staring at the fire, knowing she needed to get up and move but not able to do so just yet.

"I came through here once, years ago." Joshua slowly fed pieces of a busted-up table to the fire. "Everyone oohed and aahed at how authentic this place was. Hooks hanging over the fire grate, just like in the days of old."

"We're going backwards."

"Maybe. Or maybe the way forward is back."

"That makes no sense, Joshua."

Instead of answering he smiled at her and said, "Your ice has melted."

She used a long pole with a hook on the end to carry the hot water back outside, then slowly poured it over the ice in the fountain. Another dozen of those and perhaps the water would be melted well enough for the animals to drink.

Amber, Daisy, Texas Lady, and Fiona had found the warmest spot in the courtyard and stood close together, dozing on their feet. Akule unsaddled them and continued pouring hot water over the ice. The hot water finally melted the water in the fountain enough that the animals could drink, which they did—quite greedily, in fact. She searched the saddle bags, nearly wept over the scarce amount of feed, then gave half of what they had, dividing it among the four animals, feeding them by hand.

It wasn't enough.

"One more day, girls. Just one more day."

She didn't know if she was being honest with the animals, but she had to cling to the fact that it was possible. Alpine was only thirty miles away.

If this storm would pass.

If Joshua's foot would stop bleeding.

If Dylan's fever would break.

Too many ifs.

Dylan didn't wake as she cut away the clothing soaked with his blood. The wound stretched from the bottom of his ribs to the top of his hip. She hadn't realized just how thin he was. Did she look that way? Did they all?

"How can I help?" Joshua asked.

"I need some hot water. A cup full in as clean a mug as you can find."

"You got it, muchacha."

She wanted to laugh at his Spanish. She wanted to wail at the unfairness of the situation they found themselves in. They were the good guys. So, why wasn't it easier? Why was everything so very difficult?

Joshua waited until the water was boiling, poured it into a ceramic mug, swirled it around, then dumped it into the bucket. He repeated this process twice more, somehow understanding that she needed the cup and water to be as close to sterile as they could get. Finally, he filled it a third time with boiling water and brought it to her.

She pulled a clean pair of latex gloves from the medical kit, snapped them on, accepted the cup, mixed a tablespoon of salt into it, and stirred until it was warm but not hot. "Hold him?"

Which proved unnecessary.

Dylan didn't move. Didn't wake. Didn't crack a joke or offer his crooked smile.

She worked quickly now. Patted the wound dry with a sterile gauze dressing pad. Applied antibiotic ointment and pulled the edges of the wound together. Joshua handed her Steri-Strips. It took a dozen of them. She worried about their dwindling medical supplies, but her fear of infection won over that concern. She didn't dare close the wound with anything else. Over the strips she put clean gauze then sealed the entire thing with duct tape.

"Now for your foot," she said.

Joshua didn't argue. He also didn't scream out when she cut and pulled off his boot. Tears slid down his cheeks, but he grunted in approval. "Do what needs to be done."

"You're a tough old guy. You know that?"

"I thought I was growing younger before your eyes."

"Yeah. That too."

The foot was very obviously broken. The blood had dried, but the skin had turned purple and the entire foot had swollen to twice its normal size. She repeated the same process she had with Dylan, using the saltwater to cleanse, wrapping the foot as best she could.

"Keep it elevated."

He nodded and allowed his eyes to drift shut. Then they snapped open as if he'd forgotten something, as if he couldn't possibly rest yet. "You'll wake me if you need anything?"

"I will."

"Good." And then he slipped into a deep sleep.

She didn't know how he managed that, considering the degree of pain he must be in. But she understood that sleep could do as much to heal the body as anything she could offer. Perhaps Joshua understood that too. After all, he was a guy who knew stuff.

It might have been the longest night of Akule's life.

Each time she drifted off, she would jerk awake. Afraid that Dylan's fever was worse. Afraid that Joshua needed her. Afraid. Her fear trumped all other emotions—even exhaustion.

She stared into the darkness for hours. The sleet stopped in the middle of the night. The wind lessened.

She watched the sky slowly lighten.

A redbird lit on the windowsill.

Was it real? Or was she dreaming?

A small voice in her head said it was time to get up, to move, to begin the final part of this journey.

And yet she stayed there in the big overstuffed chair, bundled into her sleeping bag, stoking the fire with the few pieces of wood she'd managed to gather. Not ready to leave this barest of sanctuaries. Not yet.

She was struck by the silence of the morning. So much silence. Akule tried to remember radios and televisions, cars and motorcycles, the sounds of modern life—but they were fading, as was so much of what had been before. She watched the sun rise over a town that had existed since the 1800s. A town that was now deserted, broken, unable to sustain life.

"Nearly home."

Akule practically fell out of her chair. "I didn't know you were awake."

His eyes locked on hers. His crooked smile was back—less confident, less teasing, but the same smile. The same Dylan. "Been watching you for a while."

"That's embarrassing."

"Not creepy, though. Right? Because I was going more for a devotion vibe than stalker."

"You must be feeling better." She stood, placed the last of the wood on the coals of their fire, then sat next to him on the couch. Placing her palm against his forehead, she was relieved to find it cool to the touch.

"All better, doc." He reached for her hand, intertwined his fingers with hers.

"I doubt you're all better."

"We're going to make it, Akule. We're nearly home."

She nodded, tears stinging her eyes. Why was she so emotional? Dylan was right, they were nearly home. Now wasn't the time to indulge her emotions. She could do that when she was back in her apartment. When she could once again shut the door to her bedroom and allow herself to cry herself dry.

She didn't show emotion in front of other people. But as she sat there next to Dylan, sunshine finally tipping over the horizon, a single tear slipped down her cheek. Instead of telling her not to cry, Dylan thumbed it away, then leaned forward and kissed her.

"Been wanting to do that since the day we left Alpine." When she didn't answer, he asked, "Are you okay?"

"Tired."

"I know."

"Exhausted down to the marrow in my bones."

"I don't doubt it, but what you're feeling right now...that overwhelmed helpless feeling? That's lack of calories. Our last good meal was in Glen Rose. You need food."

"And sleep."

"Yup."

She raised the sleeping bag to look at his side. The wound was red, warm to the touch, but it had at least stopped bleeding.

"You've got quite a shiner there."

She looked up, and he softly touched the area around her eye.

"How's Joshua?"

"His foot... I'm not sure what even Cade could do. I hope he can ride."

"I can ride." Joshua pushed himself into a seated position. "Get me to a horse. I'll ride."

Breakfast was a piece of jerky split three ways, and a ceramic mug passed between them containing hot water with the smallest bit of tea leaves floating on top. She gave the horses the rest of the feed and when they continued to nudge her pockets, she promised, "As much as you can eat as soon as we get home. Just get us home."

Boosting Dylan and Joshua up and into their saddle proved quite a bit harder than catching them when they fell out. By the time they were saddled up and ready to leave, Joshua's face was shiny with sweat and Dylan's wound was bleeding again.

"Leave it," he said when she reached for the first aid kit. "It's only thirty miles. I won't bleed out between here and there."

She wasn't so sure.

How much had he already lost?

How was he even sitting up in the saddle?

Joshua was determined to be just as stoic. He actually insisted she duct tape his leg to the fender and stirrup. "Keep it from knocking around." What went unsaid was that he didn't plan on coming out of that saddle until they reached Alpine.

If they reached Alpine.

Now he nodded to the main road. "Haven't been this way in many years, but I seem to remember Alpine is west."

Akule took the lead, more worried now about what they might encounter than she was about anyone falling out of the saddle. No one was behind them. No sign of their assailants.

She wondered if they'd died out on the road, died from the gunshots or simply perished in the cold. She pushed that thought from her mind. They'd chosen their path. She wasn't responsible for where it led.

What a ragtag group she and Dylan and Joshua had become.

Akule felt dizzy, light-headed, insubstantial.

Dylan rode bent forward to ease the pain of his wound.

Joshua sat duct-taped into his saddle.

Amber, Daisy, Texas Lady, and Fiona plodded west, into the desert, toward Alpine.

Toward home.

CHAPTER 21

Keme rode the eastern perimeter like he had every day since returning home. He would have ridden it twenty-four hours if Tanda had let him. She wouldn't. She took the evening shift. Paco took the morning, riding it with Cade or Liam or Miles or Logan. They wouldn't let Paco do it alone. He didn't know their ways yet. Didn't know what to watch for. Wasn't comfortable enough on a horse.

But they let him ride the perimeter nonetheless.

They understood his need to watch for his sister.

Keme took the afternoon to evening shift. Akule would stop in Marathon. Leave at daybreak. They would arrive in the afternoon. He held to that belief. Told himself to give them one more day. Went home discouraged and afraid, only to fall into a restless sleep, rise the next day, and help wherever Tanda needed him until it was time for his shift.

That was the hardest moment for him.

When he first mounted his horse—a mare that was a perfectly fine horse but wasn't his. He'd pull up into the saddle, force himself to believe that his daughter and friends might still appear on the horizon, and tell himself that this day might be the day Akule would come home.

Twice he'd tried to mount a rescue party to Marathon.

Twice he'd been stopped—first by Paco telling him it hadn't been long enough. They shouldn't take the risk. They needed to trust Akule and Dylan and this man named Joshua. Keme had understood the wisdom of what his son was saying, though he didn't like it. He'd tried again the night before when the storm had hit. Tanda had stopped him as he was saddling up the mare.

"Don't do this."

"I'm not leaving her out there."

"Keme, you cannot go out in this storm. You can't risk the mare or yourself. We need you both. Paco and Claire, Pete and Danny and Little Lucy need you."

The mention of his grandchildren did it.

He unsaddled the mare.

Put the animal back in the stall.

"She's smart, Keme. She'll be hunkered down. She won't ride in this."

He nodded in agreement because he wanted to believe. What he didn't say was that there would be other people out there, looking for the slightest vulnerability, looking for a chance to take what wasn't theirs. And if it meant killing his daughter, killing Akule and Dylan and Joshua in the process, then they would.

Tanda hadn't been out there. He could tell her what it was like, but that wasn't the same as experiencing it.

So he nodded, and he went back to the apartment that wasn't his, and he paced the floor and then tried to sleep. When he couldn't, he rose, made a hot cup of weak tea, sat near the window, and listened to the sleet pelting the glass.

Hoping.

Believing.

Praying.

And finally sleeping, though not well. Never well.

He began his afternoon shift an hour early. As he rode out of town, Paco and Liam were riding in.

"Didn't see anything but a few javelinas." Paco shrugged. "I would have shot them, but Liam convinced me to wait."

"He should join the hunting parties." Liam smiled and tipped his hat. "Feels like a good day. Feels like the day."

Keme nodded and walked the horse past them and east, toward the desert, toward Marathon.

The ice from the previous night had melted. The temperature was cold, but nowhere near what it had been. And the sun splashed across the landscape giving an all-is-normal-here allusion.

The perimeter that had been established months before created a two-mile buffer around Alpine. They rode it in what might have looked like a haphazard fashion. They'd come up with a pattern that looked like lackadaisical meandering. It wasn't. It was thorough and unpredictable to anyone who hadn't spent time monitoring their movements. Even if they were able to watch them undetected, it was very unlikely any would-be assailants could figure out the routes that intersected then branched off in opposing directions.

Keme crossed county roads, dirt roads, caliche roads, and finally came out on Highway 90. The sun was sliding toward the west, the temperature already cooling. He sat on the mare, in the middle of Highway 90, staring east.

Hoping.

Believing.

Praying.

At first, he thought he was seeing spots. He definitely

hadn't been sleeping enough. He pulled the binoculars from his saddle bag, focused them, steadied them, waited.

There it was again. Not three shapes. Four.

Four spots.

Could have been anyone. He should have waited. Should have confirmed. Should have *proceeded with caution*, as Tanda was always reminding them. He didn't.

He raised his binoculars one final time. They were closer now. By steadying his hand and holding his breath he was able to make out figures. From left to right—Joshua, then Dylan, then Akule and...

He pulled the binoculars away. Rubbed at his eyes even as his heart began to race. Looked again and saw riding on the mule, riding on Fiona, riding on the far side of his daughter—his wife.

He urged his mare into a trot.

And at that moment he stopped thinking about all that had happened since June 6th. He forgot the constant hunger and the exhaustion and the terrible sadness of all that they had lost. He rode toward his daughter and his wife.

Some part of his brain realized this was madness.

It couldn't be Lucy.

He'd knelt beside her body outside the train station.

He'd touched her face, understood that she was gone, and felt some part of his own spirit go out of him.

But he also knew what he'd seen.

And he was consumed by a gratitude so great that it was very nearly painful when Akule dismounted and ran toward him, ran into his arms. Neither Dylan nor Joshua dismounted.

He hugged Akule to him.

Looked past her, toward Fiona.

No Lucy.

But she had been there. He had seen her, if only for a

moment. So he wrapped his arms more tightly around his daughter, and he told himself this was real. This wasn't a dream. His daughter was home.

And then he noticed Joshua's leg duct-taped to the fender of his saddle. Noticed the blood soaking Dylan's side.

He kissed the top of Akule's head and nodded to the men. "Let's get you home."

DYLAN WOKE in the triage center. A soft rain pattered the roof, and that seemed both right and wrong. Rain was a good thing. Water was a precious resource. Rain meant life could go on.

But he distinctly remembered the sun in his eyes when they'd...

His mother leaned over him and waited until his gaze focused on hers. "Welcome home, son."

"Mom." He tried to swallow but couldn't.

She picked up a cup from the stand next to his bed and held it as he sipped. He tried to push himself into a sitting position, but his arms began to shake and he gave up on the idea.

"Lucky you, Cade put you on one of the old ambulance stretchers. I think this thing. . ." She fiddled with something behind the bed, pushed him into an upright position, and there was the click of a lever locking into place. "Let's try that drink again."

This time he drank greedily, and she slowed him. Reminded him to take only a little. Reminded him that there was no hurry.

His mother looked different. Or was it just that he was so glad to see her? She looked steadier. Virginia Spencer looked like someone who had feared the worst, confronted it, and lived through to tell the tale.

"I'm sorry," he said.

"For leaving?"

"Yes."

"Don't be. I'm proud of you. Yes, I was worried. I was terrified when they first brought you in. Afraid of losing you."

"Like Dad."

"No. Not like that." She straightened the covers on his bed. "Your dad left without saying goodbye. Walked away for a reason that we will probably never know. But you left because you cared about someone. That's a very noble thing, Dylan."

"I'm not that good of a person. I also wanted to see. . . to see what's out there."

"And you did."

Yeah. He'd seen a lot of it. He'd seen enough to know that he was glad to be here and not there.

Cade walked into the room. "Wow. Our patient is awake."

"It bothers me that you sound surprised."

"You've been here three days, my friend. I am surprised."

His mother moved as Cade pulled back the covers and checked the wound on his side. And it all came pouring back then—being jumped by the vagabonds, the piercing of the knife, the horses spooking, Akule turning in a circle with her weapon drawn, Joshua landing in a heap on the ground.

"Akule?"

"Is already back to work—filling her shifts, helping her brother get settled, checking on you every day."

"So Paco and Claire—"

"And the children are all fine," his mother assured him.

"Joshua?"

"Is going to have a long recovery, and he may never walk quite the same, but he'll live."

He thought Cade would leave then, but instead the good doctor jotted something on his chart then stood there looking down at him. Waiting. What was he waiting for? Why was he looking at him that way?

Finally, he sighed and shook his head. "You could have bled out, probably should have bled out. I don't really understand why you didn't. We gave you a transfusion. Your mom's the same blood type, so we were fortunate there. I cleaned the wound, which Akule had done a commendable job with given your circumstances. You've been out for three days."

"Okay."

His mom sat back in the chair, closely watching him.

Cade's eyes were pinned on him.

"What aren't you telling me?"

"Nothing. I'm not holding anything back."

"Then why. . ." His throat felt inexplicably dry again. "Why are you looking at me that way?"

Cade seemed to consider.

He met Virginia's eyes and she nodded slightly.

"Because you should have died out there, Dylan. I don't understand why you didn't. I'd say it's a miracle if I believed in them." Cade looked out the window, and Dylan knew that he was thinking of his own flight to Alpine, of his wife bleeding from a gunshot wound, of being chased by the Watchmen and wondering what would happen to the two children they were attempting to rescue. Agonizing over what would happen to his unborn child.

What would he have done if Harper and Liam had been killed?

But they weren't killed.

And Harper didn't die.

They'd found Alpine. They'd found sanctuary.

"I guess I'm just saying welcome home."

CHAPTER 22

Akule waited a full week before going to see Joshua. She wanted to give him time to settle in, and she'd learned from Cade that the first few days had been very painful. Joshua needed time to rest, recover, and adjust.

Miles Turner, Cade Dawson, and Logan Wright made up what passed for a medical board in their town. Miles had been a doctor in Houston before coming to Alpine—mourning the death of his family and determined to hide from the world. Then June 6th happened. Once Tanda heard they had a doctor hiding up on Old Ranch Road, she'd paid him a visit. Akule knew firsthand that telling her aunt no wasn't an easy thing to do.

Miles and his old dog Zeus had moved to town at the beginning of winter. More than once, Akule thought there might be romantic vibes pulsing between Miles and Tanda, but then the moment would pass and she was sure she'd imagined it. She supposed it was none of her business.

Cade Dawson had sought sanctuary in Alpine, and their entire town was better off because he had. He'd practiced medicine in El Paso and lived in the barrio the first few months after June 6th. His terrifying, dangerous journey from El Paso to Alpine was what had ultimately convinced Akule it would be possible to find her brother.

Logan Wright had always lived in Alpine. Before June 6th, he'd had a thriving veterinary practice. Now he split his time equally between treating people and treating animals. He was a walking apocalyptic stereotype.

The medical board decided on placements for people who needed medical supervision. Some of the older people who had no family were moved into the local nursing home. Anyone recovering from a medical situation, who could not stay alone, was placed at the Maverick Inn, which had originally been used to help drug addicts who were detoxing.

They didn't have any more drug addicts.

They didn't have any drugs.

But the Inn had continued to be used for helping patients. Students from Sul Ross acted as orderlies and nurses, and one of the three doctors stopped by each morning and evening.

Joshua had been placed in room #13.

She knocked on his door, then opened it at his call to "Come in."

He smiled broadly on seeing Akule. She sat beside him at the little table next to the window. His foot was in a large inflatable boot and propped up on a bench.

"Bad luck that, being put in room 13."

"Bad luck?"

"Number 13. . . it's supposed to be bad luck."

"When it comes to luck you make your own."

"Sounds like something a poet would say." Akule thought of her mother and for the first time the memory brought more than pain. It made her smile. "My mom was always quoting poets."

"Actually I heard that at a concert once—Bruce Springsteen." He wiggled his eyebrows, causing her to laugh again. "Since I'm in the absolute best place I can imagine, I will take Room 13 and say thank ya."

"How's the foot?"

"Doc did a good job. As to whether I walk again . . ." He shrugged.

"You're being awfully stoic about this, Joshua."

"Is there another way to be?"

"Do you regret coming with us?"

"Why would I?"

"Because if you'd stayed at Camp Penn—"

"Not an option for me. I was leaving, had already decided that, and then you and Dylan and Keme came along. I saw your arrival—I still see it—as providence."

Akule didn't know what else to say about that. She didn't want to think of Joshua not walking. He was such a vibrant old guy. He'd been aging backward! Then the ambush. She was still dealing with that. Still woke from nightmares where Joshua wasn't merely trampled but dead. Where Dylan didn't nearly bleed out, he did bleed out.

"I have a job," Joshua said, pulling her from her reverie.

"A job?"

"Sure." He tapped his head. "Mechanical engineer."

"You never told us that."

"Apparently the Council thinks there are parts of our infrastructure I can improve."

"I didn't realize we had an infrastructure." She studied him and understood he was going to be fine whether he needed a walker, a cane, or was able to walk completely on his own. Joshua was a survivor. "But I'm well aware that you know things, so I can't say I'm surprised."

"Oh, I do—know things, I mean."

"Like what?" It had been a constant refrain on their trek home, trying to decide what things Joshua knew.

"Stuff. Lots of stuff."

"Give me an example."

"Hmmm." He ran his fingers through his white beard which had been recently trimmed. "I'm a certified beekeeper."

"You're kidding."

"I'm not. I have the certificate to prove it. I had the certificate. Guess you'll have to take my word for it."

"I guess a beekeeper could come in handy."

"Indeed. Honey is packed with nutrients, and it has antibacterial and antimicrobial properties."

"You're saying—"

"It can be used on wounds. Yes."

"Wow, Joshua. You really do know things." She wanted to stay, wanted to sit with him and enjoy the view from his window—the Chihuahuan desert on a fine February morning. He was tiring though, so she stood, hesitated, then reached forward and gave him a hug. He smelled like her grandfather, and he was smiling broadly when she pulled away.

Her next stop was Dylan's house.

"Good to see you, Akule." Virginia Spencer stood in the kitchen with beakers and bottles of liquids and textbooks spread around her. She'd started a degree in chemistry when she was fresh out of college. A new baby had put an end to that pursuit. But she'd recently picked it back up, deciding that it was never too late to learn. "He's in his room. Reading and tossing that damn tennis ball against the wall."

"It's good to have him home. Right, Mrs. Spencer?"

Virginia grinned broadly. "It's great to have him home."

Akule walked down the now-familiar hall, tapped on Dylan's door, then let herself in. The book she'd brought the day before lay closed on the nightstand. Dylan was propped up against the pillows on the bed, bouncing the ball against the opposite wall. His eyes met hers and the gradual smile that spread across his face caused her to flush.

"You're supposed to be reading."

"All day?"

"Maybe."

"I'm halfway through that book, and it's pretty good." He picked up *All the Pretty Horses* and handed it to her. "Have you read it?"

"Can't say I've had the pleasure."

"Could be describing our ride to Dallas. Even starts in San Angelo."

"It describes the fall of the world's satellites?"

"Nope. The story is set in the 40s. Or 50s. Two kids decide to ride horses to Mexico and work there as cowboys. Things do not go well."

"Ahh, good ol' Cormac. Remember, he wrote *The Road*."

"Oh, I remember. That book gave me nightmares."

She plopped down into the chair beside his desk.

They were quiet for a minute. Akule liked that about Dylan. He didn't feel the need to fill a silence.

"I'm ready to work."

"Doc says you're not."

"I hate laying around."

"Yup. Everyone knows that." Then Akule did something that she'd have never done three months ago—even three weeks ago. The journey they'd taken had changed her. She was acutely aware that life could turn on a dime. So, she did what her heart urged her to do, leaned forward, and kissed Dylan Spencer.

And for a moment, it wiped the worried expression from his face and from her heart.

Two weeks later the Lopez siblings met at a little house on Palo Verde Street. Akule let her gaze travel around the people sitting in her brother's living room. He'd been given the use of a house next door to Cade and Harper. It seemed fitting. Akule thought of Pete and Danny and Little Lucy growing up next door to Jack and Olivia and the new baby that would be born in the spring. That image could sustain her through many a difficult night.

She understood there would be plenty of those.

Life was hard.

Every day it seemed to get even harder.

But this evening they were celebrating. Her father sat with Danny in his lap. The boy seemed to have become quite attached to his grandfather. Pete sat beside Paco. Claire held little Lucy. Tanda and Akule rounded out the group, both choosing to sit on the floor.

The living room had a small fireplace that held a blazing fire. The home wasn't large, maybe fourteen hundred square feet. It was nowhere near the size of Paco's home in Cedar Hill. And yet it felt right. Being crammed into the tiny living room together brought a measure of comfort against the cold wind blowing across the Chihuahuan desert.

"Great chili, Claire." Tanda patted her stomach. "Hit the spot."

"Thank your brother."

"Paco made dinner?" Akule didn't have to try to look surprised. "Didn't know you could operate anything other than a microwave."

"Yeah, well, since those stopped working my skills have grown."

No more microwave popcorn or TV dinners or leftover pizza. Akule realized she didn't care. She could live without those things the rest of her life. What she needed was these people—her family.

Tanda reached over and grabbed the foot of her nephew. "How do you like school, Pete?"

"I like it. We get to play baseball at recess."

"Are you any good?"

"I think so."

"He can hit the ball really far, Tia Tanda." Four-year-old Danny stuck his thumb back into his mouth, something he was too old to do.

They were all coping in their own ways.

"And little Lucy? How's she sleeping?"

"Better. Paco and I take turns getting up with her." Claire nudged her husband. "Your turn tonight, buddy."

Paco groaned and everyone laughed.

It all felt so normal. So right. Problems that weren't insurmountable. Little things that their parents and grandparents had dealt with.

"I still have trouble wrapping my head around what you've done here." Paco glanced out the window. "A town council, regular patrols, hunting parties, medical teams, even schools. It's amazing, Tanda."

"I didn't do it," Tanda said.

"Not what I heard, but putting that aside. . ." Paco rubbed at his jawline. "How is it that Alpine has fared so much better than the metroplex?"

"Mrs. Looper and Harper are addressing that very question in the Legacy Project." Akule had taken to stopping by the writing center at Sul Ross University every afternoon, after her nursing shift. The Legacy Project had been created to document the days after June 6th. Anyone could contribute their experiences. Akule wanted to include their trip to Dallas—all of the experiences, both good and bad, believable and unbelievable. She didn't want to forget. And she wanted others to benefit from what they'd been through. "Part of the project is gathering people's stories who have sought sanctuary in Alpine. Describing what they experienced in other places. Figuring out what went wrong and what went right."

"As to why we fared better here than other places, I believe it's a combination of things," Keme said.

"Give us an example." Tanda leaned back, crossed her arms, and studied her brother.

"The more quickly people accepted that the world had changed, the better they made out."

"We certainly saw that in Glen Rose, and those people—" Akule drummed her fingertips against her lips. "Remember, they understood the magnitude of what was happening almost immediately, certainly before the power went out."

"Misinformation certainly played into the equation." Paco took Lucy from his wife as she went in search of a clean diaper—a clean cloth diaper. "I'm not saying that was done with terrible intentions either. Governing officials probably meant well. They thought they could handle it. Thought they could avoid a collapse."

"By lying to people." Claire walked back into the room and handed the square of cloth to Paco, who proceeded to change his daughter's diaper. "They lied to us. Thought we couldn't handle the truth. And in the space of time it took us to figure out what was really happening—"

"To separate the lies from the truth—"

"It was too late. Resources were gone. People were frightened and running scared."

"Which left immoral people—people like Will Martin—in charge. That shouldn't have happened." Paco handed the soiled diaper to Pete, who squirreled his nose in a comical gesture. But he carried the diaper and dropped it into a pail on the back porch.

Danny reached for his sister's finger.

Lucy smiled.

And something in that tableau playing out before her, more than in what was being said, settled in Akule's heart and touched her soul. They talked for a few more minutes, then Akule, Tanda, and Keme stood. Put on gloves and hats and scarves. Buttoned up the coats they'd never taken off.

It would take someone smarter than her, someone who had a bit of perspective and probably a degree in sociology and psychology, to figure out what had happened since June 6th.

Why it had happened.

How it had happened.

Akule realized she didn't need to know those things. She kissed her niece and nephews goodnight, hugged Claire, stepped out onto the front porch with her father and aunt and brother.

"This is a good place to be." Paco stuck his hands into his pockets. "I don't know if I said it before, but thank you. Thank you for coming to get me. Thank you for saving my wife and my children."

"Anytime, son." Keme reached over and pulled Paco close. They stood there a moment, arms wrapped around one another, hearts open to one another.

Akule didn't remember her father being openly affectionate before. They were changing, and in some ways those changes were for the better.

Tanda looped an arm through hers. "Your father says he saw your mom."

"I did," Keme said, pulling away from Paco and smiling. "She was riding Fiona."

"Mom on a mule?" Paco started laughing.

Akule thought it was one of the most beautiful sounds she'd ever heard.

"I saw her too." Akule's voice was soft. All eyes turned to her, waiting, expecting more. But she didn't have any more. Her mother's presence had been there as they were trudging toward Alpine. As Dylan was bleeding out and Joshua was trying mightily to continue riding through the pain. She'd seen her mother. And her mother had seen her.

She didn't need to assign a name to it.

Hallucination.

Desperate, hopeful thinking.

Guardian angel.

What you called a thing didn't always matter. It was the fact of the thing that counted.

To her surprise, no one questioned her.

Paco squeezed her arm, then turned and went back into his house.

Her father looped his arm through hers. Tanda's remained where it had been, and the three of them walked down the middle of the street that way.

Through the cold, the night, the uncertainty.

They walked, together, into their future.

The End

Already a subscriber? Provide your email again so we can send you the FREE Allison Quinn bonus scene. You will also continue to receive exclusive offers in your inbox.

THANK YOU FOR READING, ***Veil of Destruction.*** I hope you enjoyed the story. If you did, please consider rating the book or leaving a review at Amazon, Bookbub, or Goodreads.

Keep reading for a preview of ***Veil of Stillness***, book 4 in the Kessler Effect series.

AUTHOR'S NOTE

This book is dedicated to my avid readers—those of you who will follow me into any genre. I appreciate you more than I can say.

I visited and thoroughly researched Alpine, Texas and the other locations mentioned in this book. Any changes made within the pages of this book were done so in order to expedite the plot of the book.

In 1978, NASA scientist Donald J. Kessler published a paper titled, "Collision Frequency of Artificial Satellites: The Creation of a Debris Belt." This paper described a cascading collision of lower orbital satellites, something that has since been termed the Kessler Effect or the Kessler Syndrome. I have done my best to adequately present his theories within the text of this story. Any errors made in that representation are my own.

Many people were helpful in the writing of this book, including Kristy Kreymer and Tracy Luscombe. Teresa Lynn, thank you for making every book better. Also a big thanks to Glendon with Streetlight Graphics for creating covers that match what I'm seeing in my mind.

And, of course, Bob—I love you, babe.

AN EXCERPT FROM

Veil of Stillness

A Kessler Effect Novel

Book 4

March 28, 20—

Logan Wright spent an extra hour in his office after seeing his last patient. Betty would take care of the charts and the filing, but he needed a moment to wrap his head around what was happening. What he thought was happening.

His office was in the Sul Ross student center. What had been the student health center was now his medical office. It was where he saw folks who lived on the north side of town. The rodeo office was where he attended to the town's horses. At least once a day it occurred to him that he was a walking apocalyptic stereotype.

A vet working on people.

Nine months since the satellite grid collapsed.

Nine months of this postmodern life.

He tried to break his practice down the middle—four hours a day with the animals, four hours with the people. The last few weeks it had been more like six hours on each side of that dividing line.

He studied his journal, added in the people he'd seen in the last twenty-four hours, and tried to come up with another explanation for what he was seeing.

There wasn't another explanation.

The people of Alpine were suffering from malnutrition. If they didn't get this under control soon, they'd be dealing with a cascading deluge of illness and death.

They couldn't afford either.

He snapped the journal shut, reached for his jacket, and left the office. He stopped by his small suite adjacent to the administrative center. Designed for visiting professors and other special guests, it included a bedroom, sitting area, bathroom, and small kitchen.

There were no visiting professors since June 6th.

There were no classes, not in the traditional sense.

And while he had a perfectly good home and veterinary clinic on the outskirts of town, it made more sense to be on campus. To be close. To be where he could help in case of an emergency. And there had been plenty of emergencies.

He snagged his jacket from the back of the couch, left his apartment and the building. Turned toward downtown Alpine. His weekly meeting with Cade and Logan started promptly at six. He needed to know if they were seeing the same trends that he was.

Logan had grown up in Alpine. Spent all of his life there except for the years he'd attended college at Texas A&M. But this was not the town that he knew better than the home he'd grown up in. Things had changed, and he wasn't certain they'd ever change back. Though the temperature was a pleasant seventy-two and the sun cast shadows across the empty streets, he saw very few people.

No couples walking hand-in-hand.

No teens throwing a ball.

No one had the energy for those things now.

He walked with his head down and his hands pushed in his pockets. He hesitated at the door of Miles Turners' practice which was located in the heart of downtown. Ran his fingers over the words stenciled on the door.

Dr. Ron Fielder, M.D.

Fielder had been practicing when Logan was born. In fact, Fielder had delivered Logan. He'd been one of the first to die. He'd suffered a heart attack the first week. He pushed through the door and attempted a smile for Miles' receptionist.

"They're waiting on you," Anita said.

"Shouldn't you be home by now?"

"Yeah." Her eyes darted to the pile of charts, then to the street again, then back.

Unsettled. Unfocused. He was seeing it in everyone.

"Go home, Anita. The charts will still be here tomorrow. I'll send over one of the Sul Ross students to help you catch up on the files."

"Really?" A smile broke through her exhaustion. "Excellent. Thank you, Logan."

She stood, turned in a circle, then snapped her fingers. Opening the bottom drawer, she pulled out her purse, looped the strap over her shoulder. She was nearly to the door, when she turned and said, "Can you keep the meeting short? Miles is looking exhausted."

"I'll do my best."

As he walked back to Miles's office, it occurred to him that it wasn't just his patients who were exhausted and underfed. Everyone in this town was. Hell, maybe everyone in the entire world. Their society had depended on large factories, massive farms, and modern shipping to supply what they needed for several generations. Now they were facing the consequences of that trend.

He tapped on the door frame, then walked in and sank into the one empty chair. Miles sat behind the desk, hair askew, dark circles under his eyes. He looked like a first-year resident who'd been on shift for much too long. Cade didn't look much better. In fact, the man looked like he'd passed thin several months ago. He looked gaunt.

They discussed two patients who were post-op, an elderly woman who had taken a fall and was now staying at the Maverick Inn, and three children with dental issues.

"We need a dentist," Cade said. "I don't know enough about that particular specialty to know how to treat these patients."

"Maybe one will be on the next train into Alpine." Miles reached down and patted Zeus's head. The Labrador followed him everywhere.

Logan realized even the dog looked thinner, and he hadn't risen to greet him as he always did.

"How's your dog?" Logan asked.

"Huh? Zeus? He's okay. I mean, older. Moving slower, but okay."

"We're all older," Cade joked.

"Maybe that's not the problem." Logan tapped his journal, but he didn't open it. He didn't need to. "I think we're all suffering from malnutrition...even Zeus."

Miles sat back causing his chair to creak and crossed his arms. "What are you seeing on your side of town?"

"Folks coming in with sleeping issues. They're exhausted, but claim they can't sleep."

"That can be due to any number of problems."

Logan began listing the symptoms he'd seen most frequently. "Weakened immune system, hair loss, irritability, brain fog."

"Careful. You're stepping on my toes now." Cade scrubbed both hands across his face. "I thought it was just not enough sleep and worrying about Harper."

"Speaking of Harper, how many pregnancies do we have?"

"None of my patients," Miles admitted.

"And none of mine—except for Harper."

"And an increase in dental problems. . ." Logan stared out the window, at the setting sun and the empty streets. "I think most if not all of these problems are due to malnutrition. And it's only going to get worse."

"Okay." Miles drew the word out. "What do you suggest we do about it?"

"Go to Tanda. She might have some suggestions."

"Even our esteemed police chief—"

"And friend," Miles cut in.

Cade nodded. "Even she can't produce food out of thin air."

"I think we need to go south. I need to go south."

"South? Like Mexico?"

"Rio Grande Valley. Think about it. Citrus. Potatoes. Even carrots and sugar beets. It's all grown in the valley."

"It *was* all grown in the valley. We don't know that they've managed to grow anything since June 6th."

"So we go. We find out."

"And pay them with what?"

"I don't know."

Miles stood, stretched, and reached for his jacket. "Anyone want to bet Tanda is still in her office?"

"I think she sleeps there," Cade said.

Logan followed them out of the building and down the street to the police department. He had no doubt that Tanda was in her office. He also was willing to bet she would not be eager to endorse their plan.

So he needed to make her see that it wasn't an option.

He'd been thinking for months about trade routes.

It was past time that they went about creating one.

Because one thing they all agreed on was that no one was coming to save the people of Alpine. Even if there was a functional government, and he wasn't sure he believed there was, Alpine would be one of the last places to receive supplies. The feds had bigger problems on their hands—problems like New York City, Los Angeles, Chicago, Houston.

The good folks of Alpine couldn't wait on Big Brother to sweep in and save the day. The good folks of Alpine were going to have to save their selves. Which was exactly what they'd been doing for the last nine months.

Work. Adapt. Work more.

It was that, or die.

Tanda sat behind her desk, staring at the three men in front of her—three men that she considered her closest friends.

She'd known Cade Dawson for three months.

Miles Turner for nine.

And Logan Wright for as long as she could remember.

She'd trust each of these men with her life. What they were suggesting wasn't sitting well though. They'd come together as a town, shared and rationed supplies, used every resource at their disposal. "Most everyone has vegetables planted."

"Too little too late."

"We have the goat milk. Lots of fresh eggs. The hunting parties are still bringing in meat."

"It's not just a lack of calories," Logan explained. "It's a lack of the right calories. It's not just undernutrition, but rather malnutrition."

"People have survived on less. What about those people trapped in Antarctica? That was over a hundred years ago, and they were stuck there almost two years. The head of the expedition was—"

"Shackleton. 1914."

"Shackleton. Thanks, Miles. They survived on seal, penguins, and sea weed."

"They did," Logan agreed. "But they weren't well. They wouldn't have had the energy to plow a field or the mental fortitude to prepare for rogue attacks. We're asking a lot of our people, and I'm seeing the wear and tear of that."

"I'm *feeling* the wear and tear." Tanda leaned forward and interlaced her fingers, stared at them a moment. "You want to go to the Valley? Do you know how crazy that sounds? And dangerous?"

"We've discussed establishing trade routes before. I think it's time. I think we need to do this now."

Tanda turned to Miles and Cade. "You two agree with this guy?"

"I do," Miles said. "And I should have seen it myself. Proof that my brain isn't working as well as it should either."

"Same," Cade agreed.

"Not what I want to hear from two of our doctors."

Cade was the one person in the room who had been outside of Alpine for a significant amount of time since June 6th. "I'm not sure what we have to trade. I am sure it will be dangerous, and I hate to say it, but I can't go."

Tanda waved that away. "No one expects you to go."

"Right. I get that. But I want to do my part. I just can't leave Harper."

"I'm not sure that anyone in this room needs to be the one

to go." She glowered at Logan, but he simply widened his eyes and let her vent. "Why you, Logan? Why not Liam? He knows what's out there. He's trained to deal with an armed and hostile populace."

"My grandparents grew up in the valley. I know the area. I also know what foods provide the most nutrients and calories. I know this area and what we have to trade. If people are willing to give up what they have for what they need."

"I don't like it." She stood, walked around her desk, and perched on the corner of it. "But you don't need my permission."

"True."

"Okay. I'd like to run this by the Council."

The meeting broke up after that. Cade hurried home to his pregnant wife. Miles set off with his dog. Logan and Tanda stood in the last of the evening's light, backs rested against the building that housed the police station.

"Why does it have to be you?"

"I don't know, Tanda. It has to be someone, and I think it should be me."

"We need you here."

"Yeah. I get that. But if we don't do something about this now then all we've been through, all we've done to survive, will be for nothing."

"You don't think the crops here will be enough?"

"I don't."

She sighed, knowing that she would support him if that's what he really wanted. But she had a condition, and he wasn't going to like it. Best to put it out in the open now, before they went any farther down this road.

"Okay. I'll support you. On one condition."

"Name it." He gave her the boyish grin that was so familiar to her.

"I'm going with you. Just the two of us. We'll travel light and move quickly. We'll get what we need and get home."

He studied her for a long moment. She had the feeling that he was assessing her. Tanda Lopez knew that she didn't have to prove herself to anyone, but she did have to live with her own conscious, her own decisions. If things had grown this critical, and she hadn't realized, then what else wasn't she thinking of? What wasn't Logan thinking of?

They'd do this together, and maybe between them they could find what the town needed.

The one thing she knew, though she didn't understand it and couldn't have explained it, was that he wasn't going without her.

Fortunately, he agreed or maybe he simply didn't have the energy to argue because he stuck out his hand and said, "Deal."

"Deal. We'll leave in forty-eight hours."

Also by Vannetta Chapman

Defending America Series

Coyote's Revenge (Book 1)

Roswell's Secret (Book 2)

Kessler Effect Series

Veil of Mystery (Prequel)

Veil of Anarchy (Book 1)

Veil of Confusion (Book 2)

Veil of Destruction (Book 3)

Veil of Stillness (Book 4)

Allison Quinn Series

Her Solemn Oath (Prequel)

Support and Defend (Book 1)

Against All Enemies (Book 2)

Standalone Novel

Security Breach

For a Complete List of my Books, visit my

Complete Book List

CONTACT THE AUTHOR

Share Your Thoughts With the author:
Your comments will be forwarded to the author when you send them to vannettachapman@gmail.com.

Submit your review of this book to:
vannettachapman@gmail.com or via the connect/contact button on the author's website at:
VannettaChapman.com.

Sign up for the author's newsletter at:
VannettaChapman.com.

Made in the USA
Middletown, DE
18 May 2023